...ley Howarth ...

cook, geriatric nur... flower picker and ... book, *The Flower King*, was accepted as an unsolicited manuscript and was shortlisted for both the 1993 Whitbread Children's Novel Award and the Guardian Children's Fiction Award. It was followed by *MapHead*, which won the 1995 Guardian Children's Fiction Award and was shortlisted for the Carnegie Medal, the WH Smith Mind Boggling Books Award, the Writers' Guild Children's Book Award and *Young Telegraph's* Book of the Year. *Weather Eye*, her third novel, won the Smarties Book Prize (9–11 Category) and was followed in 1996 by *The Pits*. She has also written a story for younger readers, *Fort Biscuit*. Lesley Howarth and her husband have three daughters and have lived in Cornwall for over twenty years.

"Enthralling, imaginative, original." *The Times*

"Few authors could get away with writing a Stone Age book in modern street language, but Howarth pulls it off brilliantly." *The Sunday Telegraph*

"Another extraordinary tour-de-force." *The Independent*

Books by the same author

The Flower King
MapHead
Weather Eye

For younger readers

Fort Biscuit

THE PITS

LESLEY HOWARTH

WALKER BOOKS
AND SUBSIDIARIES
LONDON · BOSTON · SYDNEY

For Phil

First published 1996 by Walker Books Ltd
87 Vauxhall Walk, London SE11 5HJ

This edition published 1997

2 4 6 8 10 9 7 5 3 1

Text © 1996 Lesley Howarth
Cover illustration © 1996 Fletcher Sibthorp

This book has been typeset in Sabon.

Printed in England

British Library Cataloguing in Publication Data
A catalogue record for this book is available from
the British Library.

ISBN 0-7445-4767-9

CONTENTS

1   The Iceman – The Spook – And a Warning   7

2   My Place in Pre-history – The Fingers Family   20

3   How the Strife Began – The Amber Bear – The Pits   26

4   Hazing Arf – A Night with the Ancestors   37

5   Lunch with Argos – A Strange Dish   46

6   The Archaeologist's Daughter Again – More
    Tisane, Broddy?   56

7   Three Sisters – The First Skirmish – The Amber
    Bear Again   68

8   Down and Out in 7650 BC – Hanging with the
    Axes   82

9   The Shell Midden – Naal's Revenge –
    Understanding Arf   98

10 Return of Imchat – The Contest – An Appeal   107

11 Retreat to Mended Vision – Trying Times for All   122

12 In the Batcave – Gang of One – The Secret of
    Mended Vision   134

13 A Stone Age Rave – The Omen   152

14 Ove the Lake – Fire and Ice – The Kill   159

15 Grub Fingers Gets a Haircut – Honeyland-over-the-Mountain   169

16 The Last of Ur – Climbing the Sky – The Snow Field   176

17 Walking the Angel's Wing – King Wolf   185

18 Arf Puts His Foot Down – The Snow-hole   192

19 Alias the Iceman   201

1

The Iceman – The Spook – And a Warning

The Archaeologist's Daughter spotted the iceman right away. Wading across the ridge under Climbing Sky Mountain, throwing her ski-gloved hands from side to side, she straightened as soon as she saw him.

"Dad!" she called. "He's here!"

I was glad I'd turned out to watch. Same old skyline. Same crisp air. Same drop-dead gorgeous valley-bottom stretching away below.

The Archaeologist's Daughter didn't notice the view. She didn't notice anything except the iceman. The iceman lay on his front, his neck twisted, his face squashed. His one blind eye, like a raisin, looked mildly up at the Archaeologist's Daughter. He looked almost happy to be there. The iceman was actually smiling, his mouth set in a permanent grin by the weight of the snow which had pressed on it. The snows had pressed on his body, as well. Pickled and frozen, tanned and flattened, still the iceman looked human. One prune-like ear had the remains of what looked like hair around it. The Archaeologist's Daughter's breath steamed on the iceman's neck. A hairline – could it be? He'd been amazingly well preserved. She could even make out an eyebrow. Even – how spooky – his eyelashes.

"Dad!" she called again.

The look of the orange-brown body turned the Archaeologist's Daughter over a bit, as though the man in the snow had died yesterday. Kneeling, she stroked off some snow. Touching him felt like making a connection with periods of time so huge and empty and distant they made no sense at all. So cold, she thought; so lonely and cold and uncaring, as countless ages rolled by. The man in the ice had been washed up by time and left to rot. Instead, he'd lain a silent witness under the snow in the place where he froze in his tracks, a very long time ago indeed. She knew he was old, but not *how* old – yet. First there would be an investigation of the site. Then, probably, an air-lift to the laboratory. Finally, carbon-dating. Then they would know how old.

He could've been horrible, but he wasn't. The iceman was wonderful. A wonderfully unlikely survivor from times unimaginably distant. Her father would gloat. Another triumph for J.S. Needcliff, the eminent archaeologist. Scientists of every kind would pick the iceman's bones. He would be prised and tweezered and sampled; stretched on a slab; probed in secret places. Soon they would know how many teeth he'd lost; how old he was when he died; whether or not he'd ever suffered from backache, broken bones, malnutrition. Even his stomach contents would be examined for clues. The iceman held the past in his bones. The iceman *was* the past – a stringy orange body preserved by the snow, not nearly so horrible as it looked. Time – great, mind-boggling wodges of it – had made the iceman wonderful.

The Archaeologist's Daughter brushed away the snow. (I know she did, I watched her.) The iceman's skull gleamed. Had a winter's night caught him unawares and frozen him in his sleep? Had he been hurrying somewhere? Or had he been running away? Why had he died, alone, on a wind-scoured ridge? "Such a long time," she whispered. "Such a very, *very* long time ago."

Now the iceman had surfaced, mysteriously, through the snow and nothing would be quite the same again. The ridge, the snowline – everything – would be smaller, in some way, without him. Moving him seemed like a big thing to do. He would look different on a laboratory slab; different, and probably pathetic. Wouldn't it be better, after all, to let him lie? The Archaeologist's Daughter brushed away the snow and felt sorry she'd ever found him. She looked around. She fetched a rock. She lifted it over the iceman.

Anna Mae Needcliff, don't!

The famous archaeologist hove over the ridge. His frozen moustache steamed. He waved his arms and roared, "Anna! Did you find him?"

Nice try. I saw the look on her face. She set down the rock she'd been digging with. So far from trying to smash him to bits, she'd been trying to cover the iceman. Too late to re-bury him now. The leathery, half-hidden body looked orangely up through the snow. Soon it would be splashed over half the world's newspapers: Prehistoric Man Preserved in Ice.

The Archaeologist's Daughter looked up. "Sorry, iceman," she whispered.

Then: "Dad!" she waved and shouted. "Dad! He's over here!"

She didn't notice me watching. No one notices me, ever. That's because I'm a ghost. A ghost with a memory like a faulty rewind on the video recorder. But I can see the morning the Archaeologist's Daughter stumbled over the iceman like it was yesterday. That's because it *was* yesterday. Sometimes I get confused. I've got more yesterdays than most people have to remember. I've got the whole of recorded history for memories, me. Except I slept through most of it.

I go way back, I do. About nine thousand years – like the iceman, if you really want to know. Coincidence? Not really. One of my best friends is an iceman – OK, *the* iceman. Actually, I wouldn't call Arf a friend. More of a bad smell that hung around so long you got used to it. You even started to *like* it, after a while. OK, so I miss him. That's why I hang around the Needcliffs. I knew they'd get around to the iceman. The great archaeologist J. Simpson Needcliff *had* be in on the Prehistoric Find of the Century.

If you want to know the truth, I'll give you the *real* story behind the iceman – all the dirt that matters about the orange bag of bones in the snow. I can see the headlines now: GHOST SPILLS BEANS ON ICEMAN. NINE-THOUSAND-YEAR-OLD MAN TOTAL DORK, SAYS SPOOK. I thought I'd sell my story to the papers. Then I thought of a book.

The reason I'm dishing the dirt is that I woke up and thought, why not? I'm not exactly rushed for time. I don't have a lot else to do. Being the ghost of someone who was around nine thousand years ago isn't all a straight-cut weapons-grade flint bed. What really gets me is the things people think about the Stone Age. It kills me you can't set them straight. Take the Arturo-Chapman Museum of Prehistory, Mount Wise, Saltcombe, display case 39 – The Mesolithic Family. Schools Information Pack question 8a asks: Imagine yourself in the Stone Age. How would you cut your toenails?

Let me clear up the toenails question straight away. The Mesolithic Family did *not* eat each other's nits and chew off one another's toenails. If you get off thinking about shoes and socks it hits you straight away. The Mesolithic Family never cut its toenails *at all*, because toenails were never a problem. They wore down every day of course, with every barefoot forage – what did you think?

The only reason I can set you straight on this

stuff now, the only reason you can read the story of a – I like to think I am – smart ghost, is I write it all on to the hard disk on the Archaeologist's Daughter's computer at night. The keyboard keys rattle – pik-pok – and the words pop up on screen in the darkened, empty office. I flip on the printer (I can do that) and the stuff prints out (quietly) and I ghost it off to the publisher and the publisher makes a book and the book goes out to the bookshop and someone like you (like the haircut!) – someone like you picks it up and reads it. Once you start, you can't put it down, am I right? Talent. I'm loaded, always have been.

Let me fill you in on the platform. I'm talking pre-history, here. Don't let me try to tell you what life was like, pre-history. Eat nothing but bacon-rind for three days and have someone drag you through a birch wood in wet underwear, and you'll get some idea what it felt like. Smash a few teeth with a hammer and roll around in chip-fat, and you've pretty much got the effect.

The brushwood platform on the reed-bed was the place we always came back to. Most summers we followed the deer. Most end-of-summers we lived on the lakeside platform, those who didn't live in the sandpits. Families on the platform, Olds on the ridge, young guns in the 'pits, that was the way it went. Most summers the hunting took us over old haunts and smoothed rocks, where every camp was a whisper of every other summer. Every year the platform waited. Every year the Tribe of

Families slowly filtered back. Pretty soon the flaying racks'd fill with newly-stretched deerskins, the birch-bark canoes'd be coated with resin for last-of-summer fishing, and the platform would come to life. That was the way it was. It isn't too likely I'd forget.

Something else I'm not too likely to forget is the way just about everyone got their wires crossed, that summer of 7650 BC. That's what hurts most, looking back. I've had plenty of time to look back, and parts of it still hurt like it happened yesterday, 'stead of nine thousand years ago. But I'm jumping ahead. It's hard to explain. I want you to understand.

I'm thinking about the sandpits. Every year the keenest Horde claimed the sandpits. Up until that end-of-summer of 7650 BC, it had always been the Axes. Our Horde's the Axes. Hordes are like, gangs. Supposedly for hunting, but mainly for hanging out, mainly around the sandpits. The sandpits were choice. Amenities included a fresh-water stream stiff with shrimp, easy beachside access to kelp, shellfish, etc. plus effective control of trading. Anyone beaching a barque and crossing the dunes to trade at the lake paid the Axes a healthy percentage. Up until 7650.

The name's Brod, did I mention? *Brod* means dark man. Brod, son of Brod, son of Brod. Our whole family's called Brod, in case you're interested. I'm the son of the Brod famous for elk-antler mattocks. I should say once-famous. When he lost his job my father was a sad man. He wasn't always. There was a time he turned out the best-crafted mattocks, or pickaxes, around our lakeside home or any other. Traders would strike up the coast and blow the barter horn where the lake met the sea at the sandpits, falling over themselves to trade shale, resin, oysters – anything – for my father's smooth-handled, sweetly-balanced mattocks, worth double anywhere else. My father could whittle a tidy canoe-paddle as well, when he'd half a mind. That was about as much as he had, after twenty-odd years chewing birch gum. Just about half a mind. I can't remember exactly when he stopped making things. He'd shout and fall over a lot. Birch gum's addictive stuff.

My dad would (supposedly) go fishing. When he got back, I'd say (I'm roughly translating, here. I don't talk the same way I used to), "Hey, Dad. You left the fish in the boat."

Dad, he'd turn around. Fish? Boat? Lake? You could see thoughts entering and leaving his head without making any waves at all. "Nnrrrgg?" He'd turn the plug of birch gum around in his mouth. "S'awright. Fishboat. S'fine."

He wouldn't even have caught the fish himself. Argos the Thrower would've caught them for him and slipped them in the canoe. Dad, he'd've made a circuit or two of the lake and forgotten why he'd gone out. Making it back and not actually drowning himself was the thing he managed best.

As well as ours, most end-of-summers there'd be

around four or five families on the platform, give or take a meat-sharing partner or two. Plus the Olds, over the ridge. Sometimes the family head remembered to take over scraps for the Olds, sometimes he didn't. Mostly, the Olds went without. Every time you saw 'em there'd be one or two less. They got picked off by sabres most summers, froze to death most winters. I always planned to jump off Climbing Sky Mountain when I got to be thirty-five. No *way* was I going to live in that sabre-tooth tiger larder over the ridge just because I was old. Funny how things turn out.

Take the sandpits that year. I guess I'll never know why we left it so late to claim our camp in the dunes. It had been a fat summer. No one thought much beyond the next lick of marrowbone jelly, certainly not the Axes. We didn't really think about rival Hordes. When we did, it was way too late. What got me most was the way they moved in. I still don't know how it happened. Of course, I know a lot of things now I didn't know then. I don't feel like I've been lost in the Yawning Tunnel of Time or anything. I've been there, now I'm here. The truth is, I didn't really start paying attention until the day Needcliff took a hike up the mountain. The fateful day the twisted hide of Arf came to light.

It had to happen. Sooner or later the climate had to change, the snows melt, to reveal his unlovely remains. Arf's ice-dried leather body would tell archaeologists everywhere what an Ice Age spanner looked like. Did I say weird? Did I say clumsy, bad news, unpopular? Arf was something special. No one in their right mind could've made a hero of Arf. No one except the Archaeologist's Daughter.

The Archaeologist's Daughter found Arf the way archaeologists find most things – after a tip-off. The archaeologist himself was lean and tan, with a far-reaching gaze and a beard and moustache that frosted like a shelf in minutes in sub-zero temperatures. J. Simpson Needcliff had the kind of inhuman patience only born archaeologists have. Anna Mae Needcliff had it, too. Not that she needed much patience to stumble over Arf. He was right where the ski-party reported he'd be.

The snows had been kind to Arf. First, he'd been rapidly freeze-dried; then softly covered by blanket snows against predators. And there he'd stayed for thousands and thousands of years, until the climate warmed and the snows drew back, and Arf's time-freckled rib-cage stood out for anyone to see. The Archaeologist's Daughter spotted him right away in the thin, mean air of the snow-ridge that he lay down and died on, that cutting winter of 7650 BC, the winter we finally took apart that bunch of losers calling themselves the Pits. Took ourselves apart, too, with so much down to chance. But chance was only the half of it. I'm thinking about Arf's warning.

The afternoon Arf came around in blue paint, Vert was baiting a fish-hook. We didn't look up when he shouted.

"Vertigern! Broddy!" Too late to run off. Arf had us firmly in his sights.

"Surprise." Vert raised an eyebrow. "Arf. Dancing. What do you know?"

Arf looked weird. Antlers, blue face, the works. I grinned at Vert. Arf had been working up gods again. Arf dreamed up a new god every other week or so. The last god had been a character named Bol. Mighty Bol had required worship in the form of a stone circle, roughly on the spot Arf wanted to build a hut. Sometimes I thought Arf might be a lot smarter than he pretended to be. In the end I climbed the ridge to ask the Olds. Bol? (The Olds are pretty slow on the uptake.) Bol? they muttered, Bal? Bol? Bill? It rang a bell. It was on the tip of their tongue. The great god Bol, I explained patiently. Great god of rainstorms, green paint and bellyache. Worshipped with stone circles, freshwater shrimps and those little hard seed-pods that pop out of the ground after a storm and taste pretty good when you're used to them? Bol. Never heard of him, said the Olds, at last. Must be one of Arf's.

Arf danced towards us rolling his eyes, scattering red ochre as he came. Vert winked. Arf danced on, flinging his arms out wildly. I'd have been a whole lot more impressed if I hadn't spotted him practising with his reflection in the blue pool more than once or twice in the last few days.

"Great Naal," whined Arf, approaching sideways with many strange gestures. "Oh mighty Naal…"

"Say what?" Vertigern narrowed his eyes. He does it pretty cuttingly.

"Naal," went on Arf, with a weird kind of cast to his eye. "Mighty wolf-headed Naal and his handmaiden, Imchat. God of hunchbacks, forests – especially hunchbacks *in* forests – firestorms and chilblains. Worship the great wolf-god with sacrifice of goat's young and those little black bats you find in the back of—"

Vert grinned. "Get off it, Arf."

Arf lowered his arms. "Don't you ever think about god? The meaning of life? Why flint happens to be, like, sharp and workable and *here*? About why *we're* here to work it?"

"Nah," said Vert. "It is. We are. Face it, Arf. No one's about to bring you a roast kid goat for some no-hope god you dreamed up. Or a basket of bats."

Arf threw us a pitying look. "Why not let Naal into your life? Why not let —"

"Why not let air into your head, Arf? Blow away some of those gods."

"Laugh, why don't you." Arf stared. "You think things'll stay the same, but they won't. You think you can just —"

I said, "Shut it, Arf. Naal – pah! Imchat – pah! Arf – pah!" I think he got the message.

"The wolf-headed Naal is a vengeful god, a god of fire and ice," said Arf balefully over his

18

shoulder, shuffling off with a curse or three to spread the good news of Naal's rebirth in every heart but ours.

"I'm terrified," said Vert.

The wolf-headed Naal is a vengeful god. A god of fire and ice. The whole conversation would return to haunt me later, at a time when fire was just about the last thing anyone would throw at me. Fire and ice, a warning – and the feeling, looking back, that something we took for granted was slipping away already, even as we talked. *You think things'll stay the same, but they won't.* Just as well we didn't know it, but this time Arf was spot on.

2
My Place in Pre-history –
The Fingers Family

What was it like to live at the end of the last great Ice Age? Things were getting warmer, what can I tell you? I didn't always live by the lake. I was born in the middle of the North Sea, me. No kidding. My parents walked over from Denmark. Of course, it was marshland, then. You could take a stroll from Sweden to Ireland and never even get your deerskin leggings seriously wet, back in land-locked 7000 BC. A few hundred years after my parents strolled over from Denmark, the marshlands began to drown. They were drowning slowly anyway, in 7650 BC. It all happened so gradually – how were we to know the North Sea was rising? Anyone notice it's rising now? The land bridges melted away before anyone realized they'd need a boat to chew the fat with Uncle Bjorn next summer.

The great archaeologist J. Simpson Needcliff is *the* big noise in Mesolithic "nordic" cultures. I watched him a whole summer at the wetlands dig, turning over my old lakeside home with the kind of assurance only a prize doorknob would have about categorizing every single item. It wasn't too long before the Needcliff team turned up some Dedicated Stones (flints marked for luck, used once, then thrown away). The Needcliff team decided they were an alphabet. They even worked out the "letters". I could've straightened them out right away, but their alphabet theory was so neat and new and shiny I didn't like to burst their balloon. Same with the deer bones. J. S. Nerdcliff himself pointed out the way the "tally" markings on the deer bones they found recorded the waxing and waning of the moon. Please. The waxing and waning of Gargas' gambling debts, more like.

Gargas had a big opinion of himself. We hung out a lot together, me and Gargas and Vert. Gargas had an idea he was a master craftsman. Mainly, he wrote graffiti; usually over and on top of any cave-paintings he could find. Simps spends a lot of time on cave paintings. In his book *Pre-Boreal Hunters of Western Europe* he wonders why few stone "art" objects have survived from Pre-Boreal times, finally supposing no one felt moved to express themselves after 16 000 BC. Like, I *could* cave-paint bison on the wall, but the changing climate makes me too depressed. The encroachment of birch forest puts me off. Do me a favour. Could it be there's no surviving stone art from 7000 BC because we were swamp-dwellers? Because when we

21

carved, it was wood, maybe bone? Because wooden artifacts rot?

When I wasn't with Gargas or Vert, I mainly hung out with Hayta. Hayta's my meat-sharing partner, nearest thing to a blood-brother I'm ever likely to have. Everyone in the Tribe of Families has a meat-sharing partner. Special parts of animals are allocated by right, that way no one kills anyone else over the back end of a goat's bladder or anything. Hayta and I share neck of roe-deer, shanks of elk, belly of beaver and fox. Plus we have a non-negotiable right to any pigs' kidneys going, and the lion's share of bear's spleen. Nerdcliff lists Pre-Boreal fauna (animals to you) in his book as: red deer, roe deer, ibex, bear, elk, wild pig, beaver, badger, fox, wolves, birds, voles, fish. Wrong! He left out aurochs and dogs. Aurochs are ancient oxen. I remember Ur. Over nine thousand years down the line, the thing that haunts me still are Ur's liquid brown eyes. Did I tell you my best mate's an ox? Unfortunate, as it goes. Aurochs were easy meat. It's one reason Ur was my secret. Eating your friends was a no-no when civilization was a only a whisper in the birches.

Sometimes I tucked a wad of birch gum under my tongue and tracked Ur into the reed-beds. He was kind of calming to watch. I knew Ur was my friend because he never killed me when he had the chance – and he had a good chance – when I surprised him in the wallow, aged six. My first lake-side summer. Ur had been quite a lot smaller, then.

Even so, he could've crushed me. He could've run me down and pulped me in the clay like an old rotten log if he'd wanted. But he didn't. Facing me out over a mouthful of grass (very green, I remember, for some reason) tidemarked red with clay, he stared at me seriously. I stared back at him. The grass trembled. Ur thought. I looked. I don't know how long we'd have gone on.

Then I moved – slightly. The half-red, half-green grass disappeared into Ur's mouth. His black tongue rolled out sideways. Ur backed. Suddenly he kicked off and rushed past me, so close that the wind of his passing lifted my hair onto my cheek – ever so delicate, I swear – and I knew I'd never be so near death again and enjoy being near it so much. And afterwards, I knew. Ur would never hurt me. Not so long as he saw me coming first. Most of all, he was *there*, every summer, always – grinding and rolling in the marshes like some kind of engine, lowing like an ocean liner through the early morning fog, belching, blowing, defending his territory, siring calves, doing what aurochs do. Sitting and watching and thinking, the birch gum rush would flood my head with feelings without any names, and in that moment I'd know Ur was nothing less than the earthbound spirit of the lake. For me there could be no other.

It's not that I often chew birch gum. I can take it or leave it, me. I'm not about to get strung out on gum like the Olds. Almost all the Olds have a habit. My father wasn't old and *he* had one of the worst. Now they're trying to clamp down. Telling us birch gum's bad, when just about everyone but the Just Say No campaign indulges now and again.

The Just Say No to Gum campaign's mainly the Fingers family. The Fingers're called the Fingers on account of they haven't any. Fingers, that is. Or not many. They're real head-cases, the Fingers. They started up the Just Say No campaign expecting everyone to give up a birch gum habit as keen as a three-day fast just like *that*. It wasn't going to happen. By the time we'd had a week or two's lectures about tooth and brain-rot due to birch gum I felt like heaving all the gum I'd ever swallowed in the back of the Fingers' ancestors' cave.

You don't want to go in the Fingers' ancestors' cave if you can help it. The monster hand-prints with missing fingers on the walls're enough to give anyone the creeps. Idiots down the ages. It's a real freak's gallery. The Fingers are the only family to keep up the age-old (stupid) tradition of cutting off a finger in mourning every time a relative dies. Since they aren't the healthiest family in the world and the odds on surviving everyday life with hands like clubs are quite a bit longer than most, the Fingers keep dying. Every time another one dies, the ones that're left cut off another finger, leaving themselves a bit short of digits for hunting. And so it goes.

It's only Ma Fingers and her three sons now, and they're enough to scare anyone. Plus a few grim old aunts. The Just Say No to Gum campaign's their latest fixation. Everyone was hoping the elder Fingers would choke on their own advice and die by the end of the second week, forcing the sons Fingers to cut off their remaining digits and starve. But it didn't happen. Life, as the elder Fingers were keen to tell us, isn't all a bowl of bear-grease.

I can't tell you how good this feels. Setting the record straight after nine thousand years feels like scratching the biggest zit in the universe. Actually, I've been less than totally straight about the Fingers. It wasn't *just* that they cut off thumbs and indexes willy-nilly, whenever Uncle Flimflam or Auntie Garglejuice died. It was quite a bit worse than that. The fact is, the Fingers were monsters. It was partly the Fingers' fault the strife over the sandpits got totally out of hand, that summer of 7650 BC. Partly the Fingers, partly Arf, partly the Leaderene. Malice, dorkiness, ambition. All you ever needed for a major – I mean *major* – misunderstanding. The Trojan War was fought over less. If you've got some time on your hands, I'll tell you how it began.

3

How the Strife Began –
The Amber Bear – The Pits

The little amber bear was smooth and well-handled, someone's treasured possession. Ditto, the red-ochred mammoth tooth. In the same cache of goodies under the mossy shelf of rock, I found a sea-snail shell, a ball of coral and a tasty-sized firestone.

I took them to Treak the Bedeviller. It might have been a mistake. I unwrapped the stuff in his shelter. I held up the bear. "See this?"

Treak looked up – quite hard, under his mysterious last-of-summer hat, heavy with blanched shells and deerfat. Its gruesome edging of pine-marten feet quivered as he got up. I felt like holding my nose as the smell hit. There was something about the way Treak smelled that made you want to plunge your head in a dunghill for a bit of relief after less than ten minutes' exposure. But ten minutes, I figured, was all it would take. I watched as Treak turned the little amber bear in his hand.

"Nice piece," he grunted. "Where'd you get it?"

"Never mind that. How much?"

"I could go four, maybe five smoked pike steaks."

That made it worth ten, but I wasn't about to haggle. "Throw in a slug of red ochre, and I'll give you the mammoth tooth as well."

Treak licked his lips. "A set of three hafted daggers says I take the pot."

"Everything? For three knives? Antler or bone?"

Treak hesitated. "Antler."

"*Plus* the pike steaks."

"Done."

The knives weren't bad at all. Truth was, I was glad to have them. Casual theft had been a real problem lately. Muggings, too. We hadn't arrived in end-of-summer camp long. There'd been plenty of opportunity for casual thieving while everyone settled in. Most of the trouble came from travellers passing through to other camps, mostly kids with time on their hands. The amber bear and the shell, the smooth, ochred tooth and the firestone, were a stolen cache I'd been doubly lucky to stumble on. Doubly lucky, because I hadn't stolen them in the first place, so I had no need to feel guilty. Still, I felt jumpy. Everyone did. The Olds had formed "Cavewatch". They spent a lot of time watching to see that small replaceable objects didn't disappear. Instead, they disappeared themselves. Three were missing already. No one mentioned sabre-tooths. The Olds had been brought up not to grumble.

Treak reappeared from behind a birch-wattle screen, having stashed his bartered goods somewhere no one in their right mind would risk looking. No one messed with Treak. He was too weird. There were a whole lot of good reasons to steer well clear of the Bedeviller, and they all began with voodoo. Treak was bad magic. Anyone who doubted it only had to look at the skulls he'd trepanned. All the poor souls who'd ever gone to Treak with a headache were ranged in the back of his goat-skin tent with holes cut in their heads.

I got up to go. But Treak made a sign to sit down. For once in his unsociable lifetime, Treak had something to tell me.

"Heard the news?"

"What news?" I waited. He'd get to the point in time.

"Looks like you got some competition." The pine-marten feet around his hat swung gently as he spoke. "Word is, the sandpits are taken."

"What?" I jumped up. "We've only been *here* three days."

"Ma Fingers says there's a Horde trading freshwater shrimps in the sandpits. They dammed the stream already. Travellers, mostly. That's what Ma Fingers says."

"What leader?"

"No leader. No traps. No nets. Just a Horde bigger'n any *she* seen in a long while. They staked

28

out the dunes. Cornered the market in sand lizards already. Call themselves the Pits."

"The Pits? What kind of Horde name is *that*?"

Treak grinned through broken teeth. "Kind of in-your-face, now, ain't it?"

Unbelievable. A Horde not only *taking*, but *calling* itself the Pits! With a rush of indignation I wondered how it could have happened. How could we *not* have been down to stake out the sandpits in three whole days around the lake – the 'pits, our summer-warm camp, where the lizards were so dopy with heat you could snack 'em straight off the rocks? The Axes were getting sloppy. No one had challenged the Axes on home ground before. No one had challenged the Axes, *ever*. The most the Axes ever did was rattle a few spears and hang tough. This was different. This was *radical*.

Ducking out of Treak's goat-smelling tent, I took in the change of air gratefully. The lake stretched coolly away to the dunes. It was as fine an end-of-summer's evening as any to take a stroll to the sandpits.

Treak's knives in my belt felt good, really good, as I set out over the swamp. The coast path beyond it ribboned away to the sea, edging the lake with room to spare like an animal that wouldn't get its feet wet. Wading between reed-filled wallows I thought I saw Ur in the distance, his aurochs' head of horns like a ship's prow amongst the willows. The plump and gloop of marsh-gas wafted over the lake as he churned off through the reeds. I reached firm ground. The air sang with a salt tang already. I looked back at the platform under the mountains. A birch-bark canoe shot smoothly over the water. No one I recognized. Everything was changing, not least end-of-summer camp. Something was in the air. Something we only had a whiff of.

On either side of the U-shaped valley the hills were stiff with birches. They stood so tight on the slopes behind you couldn't spit between 'em. You can have enough of birch trees, know what I mean? That was why the Families lived on the reed-bed; we were platform-dwelling trappers, because that was the way things were. Needcliff would've loved it. Environment shaping culture. It fitted all his theories.

Theories were about the last thing on my mind as I finally made the dunes. Crabbing along on all fours a bit, I looked down on the hollow we had made our camp. Let me tell you, I soon wished I hadn't. The sounds wafting up from the shrimp-beds might've been the Axes of a long, hot, end-of-summer's evening. They might have been, but they weren't. Now the Pits had the pleasure. Enjoy yourselves, why don't you? I felt like rushing down and ordering them out, like the time my sister took my stick-man from under my bedroll and I just about shouted her head off. *Get out and don't you never, ever, do that again!* (I was a whole lot smaller then, but that's about how I felt, listening to a strange-sounding Horde in our camp – *get out and don't you ever!*) Talk about sick as a parrot.

How many nights had I lain out under the sandpit stars and woken under the dunes, where sea-smelling traders came and went?

I edged along above the slab-edged stream, to the dinner-rock, as we called it. Now I could see them clearly. The first thing I noticed on the baked-looking rocks below was a pile of limpet shells bleeding mucus over the back of someone's deer-skins. The baboon in the deerskins hadn't noticed what he'd been lying in. A dark patch down his left side showed where the gunk bit through. Limpets (as I named him) was the kind of person you wouldn't point this out to without a very large friend to back you up. Sitting next to, and all around Limpets, was the ugliest collection of weeds, dweebs, toerags and other assorted fruit-bats you'd ever want to meet in pre-history. They were almost a match for the Fingers. Some long, some short, some tall. All grisly.

The grisliest of all cleared its throat. "Think it'll work?"

Limpets shrugged. "Why wouldn't it?"

"People talk."

"Let's hope."

"Yeah," said Grislyguts. "Right."

Limpets glared. Then he said: "You got a problem with that?"

"That what?"

"You heard." Limpets got up threateningly.

"Why would I?"

"Why would you what?"

Grislyguts hesitated. "I dunno. I forgot."

Limpets thought a moment. Then he subsided on his shells. I felt a bit better after that. They wouldn't be able to outwit a heap of seaweed, if this was anything to go by. I'd heard snappier exchanges between passing sea-slugs. Casually reaching a sand-lizard from somewhere I couldn't quite see, Limpets bit off its head and chewed thoughtfully. The lizard's tail whipped from side to side in Limpets' hand. At last he stuffed the rest of it in, slowly pushing the end of the still-whipping tail into his mouth with his fingers.

I looked around. The camp was a tip, everything half done, nothing done properly. They'd hauled hunks of moss to bunk down on, but the hearth was only half built. A bladder of drinking water swung gently on the only post they'd bothered putting up. A pot sat in the ashes of a fire. Gargas' mother's pot! Shells and bones and fish-heads lay everywhere over the floor of the hollow, like no one ever picked anything up. A bit of brushwood weighted with sand between the dunes would've made them a hassle-free roof, but they hadn't got around to that. From the look of things, they hadn't really got around to much.

A girl's voice piped up underneath me, so close I held my breath.

"You. Eels. Pick anything up today?"

"A drum," another girl answered.

"Where'd you get it?"

"Same place I lifted the cookpot."

"A drum. Can't eat drums."

"I c'n *trade* it, can't I?" said Eels, witheringly. "An' that's jus' for starters. Seen that sorcerer? Over on the lake? I'll do 'im, I will. The old girl says he's loaded."

"What old girl?"

"Cackhands. You know. The granny from hell with no fingers?"

"She *has* got fingers."

"Some."

I risked a look. Two girls: one dark, one fair.

Not-Eels said, "I don't touch sorcerers, me. He puts a hex on you, you got bad luck till you die."

"So? Take more'n a bit of mumbo-jumbo to put the frighteners on me."

"Take an axe through your skull, more like. Seen those skulls he's got?"

"Might find his own in amongst 'em one day, if he looks hard enough. If he *can* look, know what I'm saying?"

"You planning on taking him out?"

"Not unless I have to. He might invite me in."

"You wish."

"*He'll* wish before I'm done."

He'll wish. The old girl says he's loaded. I'll do 'im, I will. I flattened myself in the dune-grass. Unbelievable. The murder of Treak the Bedeviller was being coolly discussed below. Don't get me wrong. I'm not especially fond of the Bedeviller. I wouldn't say we were close. But Treak had been a fixture at the fever-swamp end of the lake ever since *I* could remember, our one and only go-between in the magic worlds beyond our own.

Get out, ran the voice in my head. You heard the scam. *Get out.* But before I could move, something happened.

"I said, did you know you've got stuff on your back?" I knew that voice. Wimpish, dorky, irritatingly smug.

"Is that right?"

"Hold still. Urghh. Smells like sea-food muck from those shells."

"Say what?" Limpets (for it was he) got up threateningly a second time. He looked larger than ever standing up. "I smell, do I? And you don't?"

"Me?" Arf! Arf, with Limpets' face in his, cringing away, knowing he'd said the wrong thing, possibly for the last time ever. "Me? I smell terrible, I do. Pooh, yuk. Don't I, Cud?"

The creature named Cud looked up. It grinned nastily. "You're not wrong."

Limpets pushed Arf. "Clean it up, bonehead," he ordered. Arf bent, mumbling to himself, sweeping off shellfish, wiping Limpets' rock clean with his goatskin, checking Limpets nervously until he saw he was safe. About as safe as he'd ever be, in *that* company. Why Arf? Why here? What could it possibly mean?

"O mighty Naal," quavered Arf. "This your servant begs you, send him many days to serve and bless the one called—"

"Shut it." Cud aimed a swipe at Arf.

Limpets frowned. "Fix the fire. And quick."

Arf fumbled for his firestone. I watched him strike the iron pyrites with flint, missing more than once, skinning his knuckles instead. He cupped his hands around the tinder to capture the sparks. Arf's hands shook. His face took on an idiot grin as the tinder flared. He blew on it gently, looking around for approval. He built up a little pile of bleached-looking sticks around it. Then he added driftwood. No one spoke. No one moved to help him. The driftwood smoked and crackled. At last the fire jumped up, making the scene in the sandpits doubly strange – homely, where murder was hearthside chat; cosy, where warmth had no home.

The gruesome-looking bunch gathered around the fire. Some skewered meat in the flames, hunkering close to protect it. Others lay hopelessly in the sand, knowing no one would hand them a share. The firelight flickered in their faces, throwing bumbling shadows on the dunes. I even felt sorry for them, looking. Limpets had a year or two over me, but most were my age, or younger. Probably they were squatting in the sandpits because they had nowhere else to go. It was obvious they were outcasts, loners that didn't fit in. They didn't add up to any Horde worth the mention. And yet they were dangerous. More dangerous than most, *because they had nothing to lose*. Choosing a Horde name had been a little optimistic, but they couldn't have chosen better.

They really were The Pits.

I circled back by the swamp. The further I left them behind, the harder it was to believe it. The fire-licked faces swapped places in my mind, so I hardly knew what I'd heard and what I hadn't – the whispered talk of murder between the girls; Limpets snarling at Arf, the lizard's tail still whipping in his mouth; the moans and groans of hopeless, homeless shadows around the fireside.

The civilized side of the lake lay silvering under the moon, the birch-bark platform winking cheerily with firelight. The family would be only too glad of the pike-steaks I wore in the bag at my throat.

Distantly, Treak called, "You want some devilment potions, you come back, y'hear?"

I pretended I hadn't heard him. Treak had nothing to do with what lay ahead. Every dog will have his day. This was the Leaderene's.

4

Hazing Arf –
A Night with the Ancestors

Ask me the Leaderene's name? The Leaderene's name is Asda. (From *as – da;* literally, head of the arrow.) As heads-of-the-arrow go, Asda was sharper than most. With berry-black eyes that missed nothing, she'd got to be Leader by hazard. Hazard's doing (dangerous) things you really don't want to but can't back away from without losing face, like eating mandrake root at Treak's and swimming the lake, stabbing a flint knife fast between your fingers, baiting a stag, getting wasted on pine-nut gin, etc. etc. – things no one else in their right mind would do at *all*. The Leaderene did all the hairy things with a flourish and a berry-bright shine to her eye. Then she did them again for a laugh. She even took the lower slopes of Climbing Sky Mountain in her stride – free-climbing Heaven's Gate, a heart-stopping overhang – and returned to tell the tale. Usually, it was a one-way climb to the frozen heart of death.

No one who'd Climbed the Sky had ever come back before. All except Arf, who said he had, when he hadn't.

Arf made the ninth official member of the Axes. I insisted, at least, we made the Hazing as bad as it could be. Maybe we could put Arf off. (Hazing means making life miserable for a week for the prospective gang member. It's kind of like an initiation.)

I said, "He deserves to have it rough. We did. Why shouldn't he?"

"Not too rough." The Leaderene looked grim. "We need him, now he knows the Pits."

Hayta yawned. "So?"

"So we need a spy. Arf could be useful. Is he still waiting?"

No one had let on to Arf I'd seen his double-dealing hide amongst the enemy. For three years he'd begged to join the Axes. Now we decided to let him. The price would be high. The Leaderene considered.

"OK, we don't let him in easy, else he'll wonder why. Broddy? Fetch him over."

We usually meet in the grove. Head in hands a little way apart, Arf waited under the ghost-white forest birches that crowded away, white on white, as far as a birch-tired eye could reach. The peat under the trees was spotted with fungus, some good to eat, some not. Fetching Arf, I stepped on an ear-like thing. It fell into rubbery orange pieces under my foot. "Move." I tweaked Arf up.

The Leaderene eyed Arf over the shale axe-head she was polishing against a stone. She squinted along its edge. "OK, worm-like. Begin."

Arf cleared his throat. "I, humble and worm-like, request Hazing into the Axes."

"Our Leader," amended the Leaderene.

"I, humble and worm-like, request Hazing into the Axes, Our Leader."

It always seemed to me a little overdone. The memory of my own Hazing still smarted. Had there really been any need to cover me in honey and leave me on (what I thought was) a bear trail? So I'd make a total dork of myself up a pine tree and never be let to forget it? (Ever seen anyone covered in honey and pine-needles? They make a pretty good hedgehog.) Remembering, I wasn't about to let Arf off lightly. His torture would last a week, maybe more. We could re-write the rule-book for Arf.

"What will my Trial be, Our Leader?" intoned Arf.

The Leaderene walked all around Arf one way, then all around him the other. Many and varied were the horrible things she could force Arf to do – but one more useful than most.

"Pretty slimy, aren't you?"

"The slimiest," agreed Arf, idiotically and half-happily.

"OK, worm-like. Your Trial will be … a night in the Fingers' ancestors' cave. Tonight, of all nights. Alone."

"Thank you, Our Leader," said Arf.

After we'd seen him off we cracked up. Vert did a really good Arf – so over the top he wasn't much wide of the real thing. Arf was easy to send up; so easy, he almost sent himself.

I said, "He took it pretty well."

"That's because he keeps his brains in his loin-cloth if he really thinks we want him in the Axes," Vert said.

"It's sad. Don't you feel kind of guilty?"

"He's a weasel," said Gargas. "He deserves it. What if the Pits attack?"

"The Olds will catch it first, if they come up the north side of the lake," pondered the Leaderene, settling happily into a bit of military strategy. "If they circle the south side, they'll have to pass Treak. Anyway. The way I see it, *we* attack *them* first."

Nightfall, the whispering gallery, the Fingers' ancestors' cave. The Fingers' ancestors' cave at night was a place of drips and clunks and echoes and the kind of blackness so deep it pressed your eyeballs into your head until you thought you'd go mad unless you saw a light, any light at all, to prove to yourself you existed. Truly the scariest cave I ever went in, the ancestors' dropped away into the nameless depths of Mended Vision, a system of holes and gugs where the underground river fed the lake. Named after some long-forgotten myth not even the Olds could remember, the

Mended Vision system was mostly unexplored – mainly because no one going into it ever came out again to share what they'd found, no matter *what* they'd discovered. Mended Vision was always hungry for explorers. Some said hallucinations lured the unwary to take a wrong turn and lose themselves in its labyrinths. Others said the hands had led them on.

The handprints were down to the Fingers. The family Fingers had lived by the lake for a very long time indeed. Wintering in Mended Vision, the Fingers' ancestors had recorded their deformed hands on the cave walls, no one knew why. Ma Fingers still did it. At age twelve and twenty-four, Ma Fingers frogmarched the relevant family member up to the ancestors' and clapped their hands to the wall. Taking a mussel shell filled with liquid red ochre and a single hollow reed, Ma Fingers puffed paint over hand, wall, and just about everything else. When the hand was lifted away a new variation on the missing fingers theme was recorded on the Wall of Many Hands, for all coming ages to see and wonder why.

Some of the ancient paw-marks were pretty horrific. It gave me a kind of thrill to match my own hand with the prints, wondering what sub-human type could've made them. Someone pointed out that the wily old ancestors might've played a joke. They might've bent their fingers in and cheated. Or worn a bear's paw and sprayed *that*, for a truly monstrous outline on the wall. Ma Fingers wouldn't have it. Nothing else but mourning rites would account for the missing fingers. It couldn't, of course, be a joke. Cutting off fingers was a vital link with tradition. Why else would they cut them off now?

As kids we'd scare ourselves silly with the monster-prints, daring each other further into the cave. Most daring of all, Gargas would hide way up in a gallery called the Rainhouse, where a mineral-loaded spring leaked noisily through the roof. Here Gargas would pee gleefully on incoming Fingers, knowing his contribution to the waterworks would go unnoticed in the general rush and gurgle. Gargas had peed on most living Fingers in his time.

The whispering gallery looked down on the main chamber of the Fingers' cave. Snot-coloured stalactites dripped down on us from a horrible greasy chimney overhead. The same slimy snot-mineral covered the walls and floor of the gallery, like someone sneezed down the chimney a very long time ago. Everything was wet. Everything was cold. Everything breathed a cave-breath of ancient eons, where a drip dripped for ten thousand years before it finally ran dry.

The sheepish figure of Arf looked pretty sick below. We'd positioned ourselves in advance, screening our single candle high in a niche in the wall. Arf's candle flickered. He looked around him fearfully.

The Leaderene nodded. "OK."

Vert winked. Taking one mighty breath, he

exhaled using all of his voice, "This is the great god Bol."

Vert's voice rolled around the chamber like thirty shades of doom. Coming out of nowhere, it was a real brown leggings job. Arf almost died on the spot. I almost felt sorry we'd done it.

"The great god Bol calls his servant, Arf," thundered Vert.

When Arf finally spoke he showed a surprising amount of bottle. "The god Bol is a false god," he quavered.

Vert shrugged. I cleared my throat. "This is the great god Naal, god of hunchbacks, forests – especially hunchbacks *in* forests…"

"The god Naal is a mute god," offered Arf. "Mighty wolf-headed god of firestorms, chilblains and—"

"This is Imchat, handmaiden of Naal," interrupted the Leaderene, losing patience. "Dreadful Imchat asks: what do you know about the Horde calling themselves the Pits?"

Silence for several seconds. Finally Arf spoke. "I hope to bring them to Naal."

"What about your friends?"

"What friends?"

"The Axes. Don't you want to bring your friends to Naal?"

Silence.

"What do they plan to do?"

"Who?"

"The Pits."

"They don't *plan* to do anything. They... graze."

"They graze. What on?"

"Whatever they can get."

"How many are they?"

"As many as the blessings of bountiful Imchat," answered Arf.

"Quite," said Imchat icily. "Why would you help them?"

Arf struggled. "I don't know, I dreamed I..."

"What about the platform? Your family? The Tribe of Families?"

"The platform's doomed," whimpered Arf. "I dreamed the lake dried up. I dreamed the platform lay a fathom deep in the earth, a long time, a long, long time. I dreamed of men I never saw before, and – and the men dig, see? Dig and smooth, dig and smooth – and all that's left is dust." Arf moaned and rocked from side to side. "Dust and bones, is all. And big boss Needy Cliffson likes the bones, very good, and spearheads are good, too – and they're gone, see? All the platform dwellers, all gone and dust for ever."

"Is he weird, or is he weird?" Gargas rolled his eyes.

Arf as a visionary. I had to agree. For off-the-planet weirdness, he was more than a match for Treak. The platform buried. Men digging. *Gone and dust for ever.* I never reckoned Arf for a seer, but the things he was saying made a picture in my mind not easily forgotten.

"Very good – for the moment," boomed the Learderene. "The servant of Imchat will watch and wait. My gift to you is: *aye-muh niddy-it*. These words alone will protect you from the spirits of the cave."

Leaving a neatly-sprung coil of birch-bark to unwind slowly with many weird scraping noises, we took the snake-path exit from the ancestors'. We only just got out in time. Vert was useless by the time we got half-way down the slope outside. Jelly-legged with laughter, he threw himself down and gave in to it. "The god Naal is a mute god," he managed, speechless for many long minutes.

The Leaderene was above laughter. Above Vert. Above Arf. Above Naal. She alone had a clear view ahead. Aiming higher than most, she issued her orders with precision:

"Vertigern: to Treak the Bedeviller for three-minute poison. Hayta: with Gog the dog to smell out the lie of the land. Broddy: to Argos the Thrower for dates and advice in keeping. Gargas: to Arf from tomorrow, to spy on a spy and report."

"All," put in Vert, "to great Naal's temple for thanks."

It wasn't long before we heard him. All the way down the lakeside slope the cave-mouth brayed and echoed. *"Aye-muh niddy-it!"* screamed Arf, inside. *"Aye-muh! Aye-muh niddy-it!"*

5

Lunch with Argos – A Strange Dish

I found Argos in Ur's field. Argos the Thrower was the only other person who knew how I felt about Ur. I could trust Argos. He'd been like a father to me, ever since my own father got seriously strung out on birch gum. Argos had no kids of his own to worry about on a daily basis. Argos' kids lived with their mother, half a hundred miles away. He had visiting rights, every other month. He sent them over beads, tools, scrapers, the odd pelt of badger, that kind of thing. He did his best as an absent father.

Argos had the largest hands and face I'd ever seen, plus the largest heart to match. I knew Argos liked me a lot. We even looked like father and son; Argos' skin was quite a bit darker than almost everyone else's, like mine. Never quick on the uptake, he was quite a bit kinder, as well. I guess he missed his kids.

"Not daft, is he?" Argos nodded across the

water-meadow, where Ur grazed knowingly out of reach. "He never comes within a spear's-throw, you know what I mean?"

I nodded. "It's like, he senses where everyone is. The only time I can touch him is when we're all alone."

Ur swept his great muzzle from side to side, tearing up favourite plants like a lawnmower. His heart beat slow and sluggish. He worked on the aurochs' timescale – heavy, ponderous, massive. One day the aurochs would be extinct, but Ur didn't know about that. Ur's slow digestion brewed juices in his gut, his cloudy eye rolled, his three-ton feet browsed slow, his lawnmower mouth ground marshweed and watercress thoughtfully. Ur had all the time in the world.

I watched his black back browsing. Then I said, "I like the way he doesn't care about anything. Wish I didn't."

"What d'you wish you didn't care about?" Argos asked after a minute.

I shrugged. "What've you got?"

"Something bothering you, Broddy?" Argos waited.

I almost told him what. Instead I said, "These dweebs in the sandpits. Call themselves the Pits."

"What about them?"

"The Axes want them out. I'm supposed to ask you the best time and place to attack?"

"Is that right?"

"Yeah. So when would you say?"

"When would I say to attack? Never, unless you have to."

"We have to. Or lose out on the sandpits probably for *ever* if we don't."

Argos thought a moment. Then he said, "Mum's leg OK?"

"Not really."

"That's what I thought. Want to talk about it?"

Walking back to the platform through the reeds, I tried to take it slow. First I told Argos how Dad was a no-good, something he knew already. As a provider, Dad scored minus one out of ten. Then I told him just how ill Mum was. She'd been ill for quite a long time. Her leg still weeps, I told him. It never healed after it broke, even with Treak's snake-flesh poultice. She probably won't last another winter, I told him. I'll have to look after the family. I can't do everything. Dad's useless. I don't know what I'll do.

The hunt passed as we spoke, a brisk group of six men shouldering a birch pole strung with a broken-necked buck. A seventh man followed behind with a bunch of bloody spears. Sometimes the hunters stayed away days before they made a kill. I watched them follow the shoreline, the stag's head wagging as they went. The first two runners wore antlers to bait the stag. Usually they lured it over a hidden pit filled with sharpened stakes, jumping in with spears to finish it off. It's pretty gory stuff. You don't want to know. You want hunting rituals, read Needcliff.

The hunt meant food, at least. Our share in the meat that night would depend upon Hayta's father. We would get no share for my father, since – surprise – he took no part in the hunt. Hayta would get a share in the kill through *his* father who had, and I'd get a share through Hayta and my sisters would get a share through me. As my meat-sharing partner, Hayta carried the family, more often than not. I've got three small sisters, did I tell you? No brothers. Three sisters, is all. And a sick mother. And no father to mention.

We passed a group of gamblers over Jim-Jam. Jim-Jam's a game with counters. Squatting awhile to watch them, I found water in my eyes. I brushed it away. More came. The Jim-Jam counters fuzzed with the tally sticks and the feet in the dust in front of me, and none of it made any sense. Someone roared and won – Gargas' brother, I think. He slapped a few hands, sweeping up counters, laughing over the joke someone made about a drunk. Suddenly I realized who they were laughing about.

So did Argos. "Come on," he said gruffly. "We got better things to do."

We walked on a little way. When the laughter finally died behind us, I said, "Everyone thinks he's a joke. Why does he have to *do* it?"

"Don't pay no attention to them."

"No one else's dad's always drunk out of his head on pine-nut gin or strung out on gum all the time. Why does he have to do it *here*? Why can't he go somewhere else?"

"Probably what he was trying to do last night."

"Oh, right. Staggering through camp yelling 'head for the hills', like it's some big joke or something. Thanks a lot."

"Everyone likes a drink. Everyone chews a bit of gum." Argos jerked his head back. "You don't let *them* make you ashamed."

"I *am* ashamed. I'm sick of it, so's Mum."

We stopped along the shoreline while Argos built a fire. He built it slowly with light, dry sticks from his fish-smelling, bottomless bag. Then he gutted a single large trout, stuffing it with arrow-shaped leaves of sheep's sorrel. When the embers were glowing, Argos banked the fire swiftly with swathes of new-cut grass. Then he laid the trout on top, covering it rapidly with more. Finally I got up to help. Together we heaped and patted soil over the whole job, sealing trout, grass and embers in a mound. The fish would steam slowly inside it.

"Lunch in three shakes." Argos straightened, wiping his hands.

"Three shakes of what?"

"Three shakes of a lamb's tail. Don't you know nuffink, young mattock?"

Argos jokingly called me "mattock" now and again, after my father's (one-time) occupation. It reminded me too much, that day, of what my family had lost. After we broke open the mound and finished up our steaming, pink-fleshed fish dinner, I didn't feel like talking. The sheep's sorrel stuffing left an apple taste in my mouth. We sat watching the comings and goings on the platform a while. One of the best things about Argos was that you didn't have to talk.

Finally Argos got up. "Feel like cutting a barb or two? Only, you know, if you want."

He meant, did I want to make spear-heads? I nodded slowly. "Sure." Then I followed Argos onto the platform. The platform was shaped like a T. The stem of the T jutted out into the lake and made a jetty, the rest sat squarely on the reed-bed. The place Argos called his workshop took up most of the top right-hand corner.

"Here." Argos handed me a wedge-shaped flint with a sharp end for engraving, and a blunt end for tapping with a hammer. Then he winked. "Get to it."

We hauled in a couple of sets of antlers soaking on lines off the jetty. Then we set to work. After we'd made a couple of spear-heads I felt a lot better. After four, I felt like talking.

"There or there?" I asked Argos, poising my graver in two different places on an antler.

Argos considered the antler. It was important to get the first blow right. "There," he pointed. "Keep the graver low, all right?"

The groove and splinter technique's not as easy as it looks. Anyone can chisel a couple of grooves in an antler. Anyone can run a flint graver between 'em and strip out some kind of splinter. It's the way you do it makes a spearhead instead of an interesting-looking kebab stick. Keeping my graver low, I tapped it all the way down the antler to the burr at the bottom with the back of my axe. I did it again, careful to keep the two grooves parallel. Then came the difficult bit. Tapping carefully all the way down the ridge I'd made between the two grooves, I separated a thin, strong splinter of horn. I clipped it off neatly at the burr. Not bad. Once barbed, it might go. Argos would arm it with backward-pointing teeth. Once Argos had barbed a spear-head, it would never come out once thrown.

Around us everyone was busy. Canoes and rafts bristling with pike-gins and salmon spears jostled for space along the jetty. The platform heaved as they came and went, rocking the flint-knappers in the Gargas camp, stage centre. Gargas' family were all flint-knappers. They mainly made hand-held axes, an item Gargas despised. All of the rest of the top of the platform not being used by Argos was taken up with the women's skin-scraping operation. Skin-scraping went on all day, every day. It never stopped. The flaying racks along the shoreline were always drum-tight with skins. This year they were into bearskin. Exclusively. It had to be worn greased or not at all, with bead trim, not fringes. Fringed edges were last year's news. Shale beads were OK, amber beads better. Bearskin headbands were cool, but only worn *fur side in* – otherwise they were dorky. Henna-patterned arms were cool, too – but not legs; and it had to be the right sort of pattern. Leggings were fine, but not deerskin. Snakeskin was hot this season.

Argos sat back. "Where'd you get the knife?"

"Treak the Bedeviller."

"Nice." Argos weighed the knife in his hand.

"Not bad," I agreed. "I got a set of three."

"What did you trade?"

"Oh, stuff. The point is," I took up where I'd left off a minute or two before, "the point is, Arf's mental. I don't know why, but he's lost it."

Argos nodded. "Runs in the family, know what I mean? Arf's mother is mental, too."

"He might tell them anything – everything. You know what Arf's like. The Pits might raid us tomorrow. That's why we've got to attack."

"How many throwers they got?"

"I'm not sure. Most of 'em's half starved. I reckon ten, maybe twelve."

"Where'd they come from? The coast?"

"How do I know? The thing is, we want to attack before they do."

"They're only kids. Give 'em a break. They might move on when they're ready."

"I wish. They took the sandpits right under our noses. *And* they're thieving things."

"Tell me about it." Argos shook his head. "I kept some things to take to my kids. Nuffink much, you know? One or two knick-knacks, an amber bear for my little girl, a first firestone for my boy – plus this funny old mammoth tooth my grandmother gave me when I was a kid? I used to suck my thumb and rub that old mammoth tooth next to my ear. I liked the feel of it. Anyway. I stash the stuff away safely, what with so many strangers comin' through camp an' all. Then the other day I go to get it…"

Argos stopped. My heart raced. I felt like it might jump up in my mouth and yell out *I know what you're going to say!*

"I go to get the stuff for my kids, an' it's gone." Argos looked up. "I never 'ad much to give 'em, you know? Now I got nothing. Bit of a choker, you know what I mean?"

"Bummer," I managed, weakly.

"Anyway." Argos picked up his graver after a moment. "These Pits – what I'd do is… You all right?"

"Me? I'm fine. I better go." The knives I'd traded Argos' children's heirlooms for burned in my belt so I wished I could throw them away.

"Thing is, if you're going to attack, you want to hit 'em when they least expect it. Mealtimes are good. Wait till you see their fire go up. I'd probably come up on 'em downwind. Probably take the high ground – maybe come round by the Olds' ridge – get in ten good spears before they know what's hit 'em. Keep it snappy, make a lot of noise when you push. These Pits'll probably leg it soon as they see you."

"Right. Anyway. Thanks a lot." I undid my knife-belt so he didn't see. Then I stood up quickly.

"No sweat. Here." (Handing me a couple of hefty trout.)

I backed off, raising my hand. "We're fine

tonight. Loads to eat. Really."

"Sure?"

"Sure."

"Take your spear-heads, then. Don't want any-one thinking *I* made 'em, do I?" Argos grinned. He was just about breaking my heart.

I only got a little way when Argos waved me back. "Broddy! You forgot your knives! Hey, Broddy!"

Would you believe I had to go back and pick up the miserable knives I'd tried to leave him! The only thing that could possibly have made me feel any worse than I already did happened on my way back to the family shelter.

Something – I'll never know what – something made me take the path beside the old communal cooking pit in the gravel beds. It was a pretty big pit, hardly ever used. My heart turned over when I saw it. The feet sticking out of the cooking pit had a nasty, bluish tinge. They drew me like a lode-stone. I had to – no way could I not – I *had* to look in. The stink of pine-nut gin told me everything I needed to know. I knew what I'd see before I got there.

I reached the edge of the cooking pit. A strange dish lay inside. No one would laugh at him ever again. My father's dead blue face looked up, just like I knew it was going to.

6

The Archaeologist's Daughter Again – More Tisane, Broddy?

The Archaeologist's Daughter had a row with her father last night. It made me think about rows with *my* father. Some things never change. That's what she said. She said: I really hate you sometimes. Some things *never* change.

First she was in the laboratory. Then she was in the office. Needcliff was busy over his graphs at the time, not seeing, as usual, that his daughter wanted to talk. It wasn't a bad time to talk. The laboratory lights blazed away down empty corridors. Except for the night watchman and the odd technician working late, they were pretty much on their own. Needcliff should've talked. He should've dropped everything and taken her out for a meal. He should've done a lot of things he didn't.

I watched the Archaeologist's Daughter watching her father. After a while she paged through some of the information on the iceman without really taking it in. It was all there in black and white. Poor old Arf had been thoroughly probed and tested. Zipped into a humidity-control suit, he lay on a slab in a sterile cell. The pollen on his clothes and weapons had been carefully analysed. Even the wild grasses in his cape had been examined. Scholars and eminent people came to see him. For the first time ever, Arf was popular and famous. He'd even been named Uther by the papers, after the snow-bound ridge he'd been found on. But all the technicians called him Fred.

The Archaeologist's Daughter sighed. "What are you reading?" she asked her father.

"The anatomist's report," said Nerdcliff thoughtfully. "He was a young man. Quite strong. Tall, for a Maglemosian."

"What's Maglemosian? Nordic?"

"It's a culture named for Maglemose – meaning great dog – in Denmark. His forebears probably strolled across the land bridge before the North Sea rose."

"Young. Tall. Danish – sort of," pondered the Archaeologist's Daughter. "Probably a teenager. Probably just like us."

"I think not." Simps' tone was patronizing. "Society was quite different then."

Anna Mae Needcliff flushed. Hot with anger, she checked her watch. Would they *ever* get home tonight? They might as well doss down with the iceman, the amount of time they spent in the laboratory. Might as well jump in his humidity bag. The Archaeologist's Daughter shuddered at the thought. There was something grotesque about burying an ice-age hero in a plastic zip-up suit – or rather, not burying him at all. Ever. They were analysing everything and seeing nothing, she thought. Someone nine thousand years old deserved a bit of respect.

Carbon-dating had been the iceman's first ordeal. A tiny piece of shin-bone had been pared off and analysed. The results had gobsmacked everyone. The bone sample dated from 7500 BC, plus or minus three hundred years to present day. The body in the snow was *over nine thousand years old*. The iceman had lain centuries under the snow when the pyramids were being built. It was incredible. A.M. Needcliff sighed. She couldn't wrap her head round it. The stretches of time involved were unbelievably long.

She preferred to concentrate on the iceman himself. He was certainly a hero. She had it all worked out. It was only a question of linking all the facts. The iceman had a damaged axe, plus two skull fractures and three broken ribs. The last thing he'd done in the world was mend his axe and eat some porridge (analysis of stomach contents). Actually, the last thing he'd done in the world was mend his axe *whilst eating porridge* (analysis of cereal traces on hands and weapons).

It was obvious what had happened. Stopping for a life-preserving meal in bitter weather, the iceman had been preparing himself to avenge an ambush. Lashing his axe-head more securely to its haft, he prepared to fall on his enemies, probably rescuing smaller and weaker members of his tribe in the process. It wasn't his fault the snow had caught him out. He had lived and died a hero. The Archaeologist's Daughter felt sure of it. She looked thoughtfully through the window dividing the iceman's cell from the lab. He looked like an oven-ready turkey, trussed up alone on his slab. Was this really the way to remember him?

"Anyway. How do you *know* it was?"

"Was what?" Needcliff didn't look up.

"Society. How do you *know* it was different then? How d'you know he didn't think just the same way we do? Not *just* the same way, I mean…"

Nerdcliff removed his glasses and massaged the bridge of his nose. "You cannot imagine how different the social conditions for an adolescent would have been, purely on a—"

"I don't care. How would you like someone examining *your* body in nine thousand years? How would you like to be called Fred and have your stomach contents in the papers and never, *ever* be left to rest in peace?"

J.S. Needcliff looked at his daughter. "Really, Anna, I—"

"He was a *person*, you know."

"Of course." Simps put on his oily smile. "A person with a lot to contribute to the anthropological sciences."

"That's not what I *mean*. Don't you ever think

59

the past might be more complex than you think? I mean, different from now but the same?"

"The past is a matter for informed conjecture, Anna. You'd be well advised to remember that whatever you may think about Stone Age teenagers has little to do with the facts."

"It isn't *all* about facts, it's about the way people think and feel, the way people live together. You think you know everything there is to know, I really *hate* you sometimes. I bet the iceman hated *his* dad, too. Some things *never* change." The Archaeologist's Daughter stormed out.

Later I found her crying in her bedroom.

Anna Mae Needcliff, don't!

How to tell her crying wouldn't change a thing? So far from being a hero, Arf had died as he'd lived – in weirdsville. Apart from a hiccup over Arf, the Archaeologist's Daughter was more nearly right about everything else than she knew. The distant past *was* more complex – and sadder – than anybody dreamed.

"Take this." My mother handed me her best and only cookpot, wrapped in bitter leaves of rue. "You'll probably find her up the ancestors'."

"But why?"

"We have to thank her formally."

"With our only cookpot? What for?"

"Because it's the thing to do." My mother put on her hard face. "Ma Fingers laid out your father. We have to give her something."

My three small sisters looked on, interested I was actually arguing. Usually I don't bother. I looked at my hard-faced mother. Pride was all she had left. She'd lost the so-called breadwinner, she wasn't about to lose face as well. I took up the leaf-wrapped cookpot and tucked it under my arm. Some breadwinner. This would be the last thing I would do for my father. I was breadwinner now.

The bitter smell of rue for regret sharpened my thoughts all the way up to Mended Vision. Missing my father was a new kind of feeling for me. I had to think hard about his good points. There *was* a time he'd been sober. I had a feeling his funeral was one thing he might've approved of. Simple, plain, no fuss – the way he'd been himself in my distant memory, in the childish days before birch gum. Funeral rites at short notice? Nothing could be simpler, decided the Burial Committee chairman, calling the Committee to order with his ceremonial hammer. The cooking pit would simply be filled in following the appropriate rites, and a new one dug when everyone felt like doing it. They would let matters lie. Literally. After much wailing and gnashing of teeth and sprinkling of red ochre over body, grave and just about everything else, the old man was pretty much laid to rest, bar the shouting. The only thing that got me was the swan's wing. I'd managed OK until then.

Tenderly unwrapping the swan's wing, my mother had laid it in the grave under my father's head. It was a real shock. I hadn't had any idea she loved my father the way you do when you make a gesture like that. Pillowed on white feathers, the old man looked more angelic than he ever had in his lifetime. It was a nice touch. One that found water in my eyes.

The black hole of the Fingers' ancestors' cave widened very slowly as I climbed. I hadn't been near it since Arf's Hazing. Visiting the cave had been a joke, then. Now it was just a drag. Just about the last person I wanted to see in the world was Ma Fingers. Ma Fingers was a real ghoul. She wore her hair wound round a bone on the top of her head, in a greasy flat saucer like a bracket fungus. When she wasn't being a secret, black and midnight hag – which she was, most of the time – she did a bit of undertaking on the side. No one knew what else she did. It was a mystery what she found to do up the ancestors' cave so many days. Some days Grub went too. Ma Fingers had three sons – Grub, Stub and Falco – all as ugly as each other. They all wore the bracket-fungus topknot, they all had missing fingers. Some said Ma Fingers lived off bats. Others said she changed into one at night and flew around carrying off babies in their sleep, etc., etc. It didn't matter to *me* what she did up there, I wasn't about to pay her a social call. Ma Fingers had prepared my father's body for burial. I had to take her a gift and that was that. I could always leave the cookpot outside and leg it. I didn't *have* to go in.

It turned out that the cave-mouth had quite a bit

to say, well before the gloom sketched me out Ma Fingers and a tall, thin girl with a voice I'd heard before. The last voice the cave had thrown around had been Arf's. These two were quite a bit more interesting:

"So, when?" asked the girl. (The murderous voice from the Pits. Wasn't its owner called Eels?)

Ma Fingers said, "When I tell you. What d'you take me for?"

"A greedy, back-stabbing old crone," said Eels. "Isn't that what you are?"

"I know when to give the signal," growled Ma Fingers. "I just 'ope you know what you're up against."

"Everything's sweet. Just give us the nod when the men's away."

"I 'ope you can take the whole camp. They don't *all* go off on the hunt."

"It won't come to that, we got plans."

Ma Fingers nodded. Then she thought of something. "And listen here, there's things I want when you raid 'em, see? Special things." She brought up a claw-like hand, tapping Eels' chest for emphasis. "I want the Burial Committee hammer out of the Chairman's camp. It's a nice piece, that 'ammer." Tap, tap. "I want the Gargas family bearskin – " tap, tap, "*and* the beads you'll find there – first bender on the shoreline behind the flaying racks. And when you do the Bedeviller, I want his last-of-summer hat."

"Anything else?" Eels coolly side-stepped the

tapping claw.

Ma Fingers narrowed her eyes craftily. "Broddy Brodson's mother got a 'markably fine cookpot. I wun't mind that, if you're passing."

Eels watched Ma Fingers' face. Suddenly she said, "Well, now, we'll have to see what we can do, won't we?" Just as suddenly, she swung out into the sunlight.

"Off then, dearie, are we?" Ma Fingers moved out of the shadows, shading her eyes against the sun, peering after Eels as she slipped away through the trees. "See you soon," she called hopefully.

I watched Eels swinging easily away down the slope, not looking back, unhurried, unworried, with nothing to lose. What was it like to be rootless and free? With no one to care if you lived or died, if you lied or murdered or cheated? What was it *like* to hit bottom? I counted a-hundred-fishes-jump-twenty-times-over-the-weir. It took me quite a long time. Then I climbed up to the cave-mouth. Just my luck – Ma Fingers spotted me right away.

"Well, now – Broddy Brodson." The honeyed tones made me want to gag. "Did you just arrive?"

You might well ask, I thought, *you two-faced bag of bearfat.*

"My mother sends you this gift on behalf of my father's decease," I announced formally, setting down the leaf-wrapped cookpot – the very cookpot Ma Fingers planned to take by murder and betrayal.

"What have we here, I wonder?" Ma Fingers

kept up the act as she peeled away the rue-wrapping. "Oh – she shouldn't have – such a *very* nice handle. Don't you think? A *very* handsome cookpot. Well. It's more than generous of her, tell your mother."

I thought so, too. Considering. I turned to go, but Ma Fingers was surprisingly quick to stop me. Slipping her arm through mine and taking hold – actually pinching my flesh with her claw – she said, "Take a drink with me, Broddy. You'll be thirsty after your climb."

She made it pretty difficult to refuse. The tisane, or herbal tea, she gave me out of a pitcher was kind of warm and sickly, especially drunk in the airless atmosphere inside the cave. I felt like I couldn't breathe. She made me sit down awhile. Truth to tell, I was glad to.

Ma Fingers sat close – too close – beside me. "And how's your poor mother?" she asked.

"OK, I suppose. Could be better."

"Her leg'll be playing her up?"

"A bit," I told her, guardedly.

"You'll have given up birch gum, of course?"

I shrugged. "Never been into it, really."

"That's the way. Your father's a terrible warning to us all."

"I guess." Self-righteous old buzzard, I thought.

"And your three poor sisters. Who's got your three poor sisters?"

"No one has. They're with Mum."

"There. Here was I thinking she'd be giving

them over to a family with a provider."

"Well, she isn't. I'm the provider now."

"Are you now? Well, well, well. Well, well, well, well, well."

Ma Fingers' countless "wells" seemed to drill me into my seat. She said a lot more I don't really remember, keeping her voice soft and low so I had to strain to catch what she said. After a while she got up. She seemed keen to show off the Wall of Many Hands. I sat back and let her. I didn't feel much like getting up myself.

"This here –" pointing to an elephant-man handprint near the roof "this one here's one of the oldest. Notice the way three of the fingers are missing their top joints? We're much more thorough these days. We take the whole finger off, clean as you like. More tisane, Broddy?"

She jumped down and handed me the pitcher. A musty – not unpleasant – smell wafted up from the pale green tisane inside. It made me want to drown in it. I drank and drank and drank.

Ma Fingers began to stroke me with her voice, gently, over and over, "You want to build yourself up; your poor, dear mother's going to need all the help she can get. Your poor unfortunate mother … three poor fatherless girls … and your poor dear father himself, of course … we must always remember your father … poor mother … poor sisters … poor father…"

The gloom of the cave seemed to thicken around her. Something gleamed in her hand. "We must remember your father … mustn't we? Your poor … dear father. You'll want to remember your poor, dear father properly, now won't you? And these days it doesn't hurt a bit."

Clamping my right hand to a stone, she separated the fingers. I watched dully as she raised her arm. It really was quite a big knife. More like a machete, really. It would make short work of a finger, anyone could see. I watched the big flint knife hover over my hand. I watched her tense her arm to bring it down.

Suddenly everything changed. I'm still not sure how it happened. Suddenly a big, messy dog was jumping up over everything, dashing the pitcher of tea over, barking with excitement, sending Ma Fingers' big flint knife ringing across the cave floor. A big, joyful, messy dog, smelling of fields and hills and sunlight – and behind him, Hayta, dear Hayta, the best and only blood-brother I'm ever likely to have.

"Come on, Broddy," said Hayta. "Come and see what we found! Who's for a race to the lake?"

"I am," I said, in a dream. "I'll come with you, Hayta," I said. "I'll come with you."

7

Three Sisters – The First Skirmish – The Amber Bear Again

Let me tell you about my sisters. First up, has to be Broddha. She's the eldest of three. Still miles younger than I am, Broddha's eight, OK? After her comes the Beast. That's what I call her, always have, mainly because she bites. My middle sister's real name is some female version of Brod – Brodil, I think she was named. Anyway. The Beast's six and no one calls her Brodil. Ever. After the Beast comes Bee. Bee's only four.

The reason I didn't see a whole lot more of my sisters around the time my father died was that I was always out foraging for food. No surprises there. The idea of being family provider after the old man went belly-side up was no big wows for me. One way or another, I'd been providing more years than I could remember. So just about the only quality time I ever spent with my sisters was early mornings and evenings. Mornings, the Beast would sit dangling her feet off the platform as dawn broke and the mist rolled in off the sea and the kites wheeled above on air currents warming in the almost-risen sun.

Sometimes Bee would wake up. "Is it light yet?" she'd ask, automatically. Always the same question, in exactly the same tone of voice. "Is it light yet?" Always the Beast'd growl back: just-about-light-go-to-sleep.

It never really was. Light, I mean. Always the dawning sky was tinged with the last-of-night and the kind of very pale yellow you find in the face of a primrose, when the Beast and I had our talks. The odd salmon jumped in the lake. Birch-bark floats bobbed on hidden nets, way out under the mist. Often Ur lowed, frighteningly – a broken, blurting, foghorn-sound, throwing itself out across the lake, echoing off, forever, into the mountains. It made you think of lonely things. The mountains, and what lay beyond them.

It was then that the Beast and I would talk. We'd talk about Climbing Sky Mountain. No one knew what lay on the other side of Climbing Sky Mountain, because no one ever climbed it unless they were mad or dying, or both. The way lay past the Laying-out Ground of the Dead, where red-beaked kites cleaned the bones of relatives long since perished. They were real experts, those kites. Sometimes you'd see 'em high in the sky with a bone, dropping it – crack – for the marrow. Good old Uncle Gastergrass, you'd think. Looks like he Climbed the Sky. My dad never Climbed the Sky.

His spirit would never fly with the kites. Instead, it would haunt the cookpit. No one would ever feel comfortable there again.

When the Beast and I talked about the mountain, usually she'd start, "And there's bears over there with tan coats like I like, very, *very* light brown? An' I don't hardly do no scraping on 'em at all, the skins're so nice an soft an' fluffy – an' there's millions of beads already on so I don't have to sew 'em at all..."

"Wait a minute. That's silly. You don't get pelts with beads already on. Not even over-the-mountain."

"It's *my* over-the-mountain say, an' they *are* on already if I like. An' there's honeycomb honey I reach in an' get with not even one sting on my arm. An' over there it's honey *every* day."

It was just a dream, and she knew it. The land beyond Climbing Sky Mountain was probably just like our land, the land of the lake. It didn't hurt to dream. But sometimes she went a lot further.

"An' when Mum goes over the ridge I'm goin' there, see?"

"What?"

The Beast splashed her feet. The water was pretty scuzzy off the birch-bark platform. Fruit peel, flaying waste, rags and tatters of skins, bones and scraps of food, flint-ends, wood shavings, feathers, tallow, antler discards, nut-husks, jaw-bones, lumps of resin – even strips of pigs' intes-tine, bloated by the wind – everywhere we went,

70

we messed up. Fish-heads heaved in the shallows on a slight – a very slight – swell. Local pollution was getting to be a real problem.

"When Mum goes an' lives on the Olds ridge, Bee an' me's goin' over Climbing Sky Mountain an' you're not," the Beast repeated.

The Beast had a winning smile. Most times, she'd win me around. But the times she started round the mountain, even in her head, were the times I knocked her back. Someone had to. She was only six, after all.

"Look. You don't go anywhere without me or Mum, OK? Not Climbing Sky Mountain, not Mended Vision, not the other side of the lake."

"I *will*. An' me an' Bee's *goin'* when we want to."

Stubborn little number, or what? I felt like shouting at her. "Want to know why most people don't come down from the mountain? Because they freeze to death. It's always snow up there."

"It *is* always snow, an' they like it – an' they never come down again 'cos when they get to honey-land they never, ever want to come back."

"Don't be stupid. I've been there anyway," I lied. "Argos took me once. The other side of Climbing Sky's jus' the same as this."

The Beast looked coolly into my eyes. "Gimme a break," she said.

Why I'm remembering all this now is, those early-morning talks with the Beast on the edge of the birch-bark platform could've told me a lot if I'd listened, probably more than the ritual sign in the middle of the path Hayta stumbled over, the morning Ma Fingers cast her spell over me under the Wall of Many Hands. That strange, rue-smelling morning Hayta and I raced down from the Fingers' cave with the sun and the wind in our faces, I felt like I was floating. Hayta pulled me after him. See what I found. Run. Threading the lakeside willows, we finally reached the weird-looking stick in the path.

"What is it?" asked Hayta, over the thin wand of willow tipped with stoat's tails. Winter stoat, it was. "Think it's a warning or something?"

"Willow and ermine." It smelled disgusting, whatever it was. Kneeling to examine Hayta's find, I still felt kind of woozy. The run from Mended Vision had cleared my head quite a bit, but I didn't want to think about what had almost – not quite – gone down with the big flint knife. Hayta didn't either. He hadn't said a thing. The sunlight kissed off Ma Fingers' spell. Had it really happened? "Could be a challenge. Maybe."

Hayta looked doubtful. "Better leave it alone."

I pulled it out. It was neatly crafted. Deliberate. Someone had stuck the willow wand in the middle of the path. Made a circle of stones. Sprinkled it ritually with ochre. "Why?"

Hayta shrugged. "Bad magic."

"How about the Pits' camp?" I asked after a moment. "You been over there lately smelling the wind?"

"Gog has," said Hayta fondly, nudging the old brown dog with his leg. The old brown dog looked up lovingly. Hayta teased her ears. Soft name, soft dog. Hayta loves her like elvers. That's what he says. Like freshly-wriggling elvers, lightly poached for breakfast. What's that supposed to mean, I asked, laughing. You can't love a dog like your favourite food. Why not, said Hayta carelessly, opening his arms to include just about everything *else* he loves. You can't help but like him, and that's the truth.

"And?"

Hayta hesitated. "There's something up, all right. They're tooling up for a fight."

"How many throwers?"

"A dozen."

A dozen was bad. About as bad as it could be.

"They're waiting on the nod from Ma Fingers," I told Hayta. "No kidding. Ma Fingers is pond-scum. I overheard the plan."

Gog the dog rumbled threateningly. Someone was coming, someone she didn't like the smell of a whole lot. No wonder, I thought, when I saw. The undying enemy of dogs everywhere, at all times, ran easily through the willows. Without breaking her stride the Leaderene took a swipe at Gog. Reaching us, stopping, she touched Hayta's arm. "What's your hurry getting here? What gives?"

I showed her the willow-wand. "This."

"Ugh. Stinks of Treak. So?"

Treak. Of course. But why? The Leaderene set

her hands on her hips. A full quiver of arrows, tipped with the wafer-thin flint arrowheads Needcliff so loved to find and clean and label, showed their flight feathers over her shoulder. She had on full battle drag. I wondered why. The Leaderene in warrior-maiden mode was no small sight to see.

"So Hayta just found it. What's it mean, d'you think?"

But the Leaderene's mind had moved on. "There's trouble in the gravel beds. We need to get over there. Now."

"What *kind* of trouble?" Hayta looked worried. Hayta likes everyone to be happy. Peace, love and understanding. Everyone. All of the time.

"How many kinds are there? I saw Grub Fingers heading over with a spear. I think the Pits are stirring it. Let's go."

"Better get Argos," I panicked. Argos is an honorary Axe. Always handy in a push, having someone on your side three times bigger than anyone else, I find.

"Someone got him already."

The Leaderene loped off. Hayta followed, then me. Gog the dog ran annoyingly behind and alongside, making rushes ahead, sometimes getting mixed up in my legs, sometimes not. The hot pace cleared my head completely. Our Leader could make throwing a stick seem like work.

We jogged along in silence, then, "Where's Arf?" she threw over her shoulder.

"In the river," answered Hayta.

The Leaderene grimaced. "Where else?"

We passed him on the way, the nerd. The ice-chilled river tumbling down from Climbing Sky fed the lake where the gravel beds met the swamp. It made the gravel beds *into* the swamp. It's fan-shaped delta made a gloomy marsh not much good for anything but Treak's nasty goatskin bender and a million mosquitoes. Along the ice-chilled river we came upon Arf.

We crossed upstream as quietly as we could, carrying Gog, badly wanting to laugh. Completely unaware of anything but his own idiotic reflection in a still, small backwater under a rock, Arf was enjoying himself. First he admired his reflection. He struck a few fierce-looking poses, rolling his eyes and baring his teeth. Then he sprang backwards, then sideways, three times. Hayta doubled up. Too much. Arf snuck up on his reflection again, singing now, a mixed-up version of Treak's Ghost Chant. He stuck out his blue-streaked tongue. For a while he pulled faces, trying different profiles, arguing with himself. When Arf started up with the strange gestures and the leaping sideways again, Hayta kind of exploded and we had to hurry away.

"What's he *on*?" The Leaderene rolled her eyes. "We're relying on *him* for a spy in the enemy camp? What are we, desperate?"

"He likes dancing," I said. "It's just the way he is. But I wouldn't rely on him for anything. I wouldn't even—"

"Listen." The Leaderene held up her hand. "There. Hear that?"

Angry voices – Treak's, for one. Nasty-sounding laughter, somewhere ahead to the right. The outline of someone – Grub Fingers – his back to us, watching in the trees, was more than a little unsettling. The Leaderene took it in quickly. We were running, then – I wished we were running away – and everything happened at once.

First, there was Treak with a stick. A stick like the one in the path. Then there was Limpets. And Cud. Quite a few more behind Cud. No one moved. No one spoke. Everyone watched and waited. Treak spat out a plug of birch gum. Eyeing Limpets, he bent and screwed a willow-wand, like the one we found earlier, in the path. He sprinkled it with ochre. He made a line across the path at each side of the stick with his staff. Then he folded his arms.

"Cross this line," he sneered. "Make my day."

Treak's last-of-summer hat had been stuck with quills, freak roots and birch twigs. A whole pine-marten's face had been added over his forehead. The niffy goatskins he usually wore had been replaced by his ritual costume of a whole black bear's pelt hung with small unfortunate animals' skulls. His face and the whole length of his Bedeviller's staff were thickly ochred red. His red legs disappeared into bear's feet boots. He looked like everyone's worst nightmare – which was, after all, the whole point.

"Say that again," fronted Limpets, a little uncertainly.

"I said, make my day." Treak brought out a rat's tail. Dipping it into a pot at his waist, he flicked it in three directions, one of them Limpets'.

"What *is* that?" Limpets sniffed suspiciously.

Treak closed his eyes. "All boundaries sealed," he intoned, swaying ever so slightly. "Bad magic and a withered liver on those who break the bounds. Cross this line and die."

"We walk where we want to, we take what we want. Tell *that* to the Axes," hissed Cud.

Limpets turned. "Where's Spider? Hey, Spider. See that line? Cross it, will ya? Now."

Cud collared a stick-like creature made of all the bits nobody wanted when people were first invented. It had ritual scarring on its arms and a helmet of mud-plastered dreadlocks. It didn't look much like a spider. "I don't want no withered liver," it whined. "Cross it yourself, why don't you?"

"You saying I couldn't?"

"I'm not saying nothing."

"And I am?"

"Am what?"

"What I said." Limpets stared madly at Spider.

It was the kind of no-win repeat loop Limpets seemed to enjoy. Everyone waited to see what would happen. No one seemed keen to cross Treak's voodoo line – not now, at least – no matter how much they posed behind it looking cool.

Limpets poked Spider. Spider poked him back. Everyone else made a circle. It might have been – I don't know – a way of saving face.

Hayta nudged me. "Argos."

Argos approached at a rapid jog, bristling with the full complement of spears for every occasion. He ran smoothly up to, and into, Cud. Then he stopped.

"This lot giving you trouble?" Argos picked Cud up lightly.

"Kind of," I told him, breaking sweat with relief.

"What was that you said earlier?" the Leader-ene asked Cud. "Something about taking whatever you want?"

"Taking – taking what *other people* don't want." Cud smiled crookedly. "Recycling rubbish. Rags, bones, bear-grease, flaying waste. You should see our camp. We're regular recyclers, us."

Limpets nodded. "Right. Like he said. Environ-mentally friendly, that's us." He re-arranged his face into what passed for a smile. "We were just on our way. This Treak guy's cool. Never wanted to walk here, anyway. And now we say goodbye. Goodbye."

"Wait up." The Leaderene rammed her spear into the ground between Limpets' feet. The shaft thrummed. Limpets jumped. It was a ritual move. There could be no mistaking what it meant. The Leaderene cleared her throat, "The Axes challenge the Pits by Force of Hand in the Open. Any day.

Winners take the sandpits, losers vacate."

Now it was out. The formal challenge sat there and waited. "Excuse me!" Limpets shrugged. "We don't have time for this."

"Trial by Force of Hand," put in Argos, who usually invigilated Trials, "is a serious matter, so it goes…"

"What Test?" pressed the Leaderene.

"No Test." Limpets grinned. "We got the sand-pits already."

"Not for long, dogsbreath."

"Challengers set time and place. I want a good, clean contest, one to one, with – wait a minute…" Argos stared at Treak. "What's that you got round your neck?"

"What?" Treak examined his chest irritably.

"That little amber bear." Argos tore it off. He turned the little amber bear slowly in his oversize hands. Then he looked up. "You better 'ave a good reason you got this." Argos' voice was flat and deadly. "I'm asking you one time: Where'd you get this?"

"Hey." Treak spread his red hands in a mollify-ing sort of way. "Hey, big guy. Nobody got noth-ing they didn't oughta. Tell it to Broddy Brodson."

"Broddy Brodson? Why?"

Treak shrugged. "He brings me a straight trade. Bunch of little trinkets – amber bear included – against a set of three 'ceptionally fine antler knives. Real steal for the kid, I don't know why I do it."

"Broddy wouldn't do that." Argos looked like

thunder. "Don't lie to me, magic man."

"Why would I? There he is." Treak pointed. "Ask him yourself, why don't you? "

A real steal for the kid. Argos turned slowly. The look in his eyes half killed me.

"Broddy," he said. "What's this?"

"Argos, I took 'em, then I realized – I wanted to tell you, but it was kind of too late, and I had the knives already…"

Argos' eyes never left my face. "You took the things for my kids. When did you take them?"

"Ages ago now, but I didn't know at the time…"

"You didn't know at the time," repeated Argos, "but you know now."

"Can we, like, wrap this up?" Limpets and Cud pushed through. The whole rat-pack followed on, spinning me one way, then the other, as they went. I felt a lot like going with them. Instead I started running.

"Broddy! Come back!" I thought I heard Argos. It made me run even faster.

I half turned when I reached the woods – catching Argos searching after me with (what I knew were) hurt-filled eyes. I saw him look up, then down. I saw him shake his head. Then I turned away, running blindly from everything I couldn't – wouldn't – be able to explain in a million years. Like how you betray your best friend. Why hadn't I tried to explain? Made amends, somehow? My heart jumped. The pits, or what? Join the den of thieves in the sandpits, why don't you? You qualify, and then some.

It was true I hadn't known the cache of treasures under the rocks belonged to Argos at the time. But I might've known it had to belong to *someone*. Everything that was going to had caught up with me. Wishing I didn't care about anything ever again, even – especially – self-respect, was just about as near to grieving for Dad as I was ever going to get. Running madly, uncaringly, fast as I could, through the woods, I surprised a young roebuck rubbing velvet from its antlers on a stump. We stared at one another in a less dangerous re-run of my introduction to Ur. The hanging velvet on the buck's antlers swung very slightly as he looked at me, the birch woods whispered behind. Then the buck kicked off through the trees. I took the opposite direction, leaping, dodging, slapping from trunk to trunk, hurting my hands, knees, feet, weaving recklessly through the birches – straight into the arms of Grub Fingers.

Grub Fingers smiled. His disgusting breath hit my face. Then he closed his three-fingered hand on my arm as though it were a ripe fruit he'd been waiting a long time to pick.

8

Down and Out in 7650 BC – *Hanging with the Axes*

Eee-agh! Eee-agh! Eee-agh-*agar!*

We all pushed together on the word, the pine logs rocking, then teetering, then thundering off down the ridge, pounding and smashing and shattering anything in their path. Way below on the flank of the slope, the Olds' camp waited unknowingly like the last sitting duck on the pond. *Watch out below!* It was kind of fearsome, the thing we'd set in motion. Too late to wind it back now. I checked Limpets – real name Viger Wildgoose. Viger Wildgoose grinned. The word was hit, then run.

Those were big pine logs. We all crowded round to see what would happen when they hit, Cud's body odour problem flavouring the moment in a way it was hard to forget. Those logs jumped and smashed their way down the slope, pounding the Olds' camp to tinder-wood and wiping it off the ridge like it had never existed, sweeping hut-bases, flaying racks, bird-coops and all, over and down to the lake-edge in a mess of splintering stakes and spinning, hard-edged bender-pegs. After they finally all finished up at the bottom there was a silence. Then the wailing began.

I said, "I thought the Olds were supposed to be off at some fish-fest."

"Like, it makes a difference?" Cud smiled like the snake that just swallowed a goat. "What's with you? Cold feet?"

"No colder'n yours. What now?"

"What now?" Cud mugged, making me want to park my fist in his face. "What now? Now we move in."

We moved in quickly. No one challenged us. Everyone scattered. We poured down that slope like a flash-flood, giving it the Pits' war-cry as we came. Some old goat almost had a heart-attack trying to untie his scabby old dog and leg it before we got there – it was kind of pathetic to see; also the old girl doing a runner with a full basket of quail chicks looked so much like a frightened chicken herself, it would've been funny if we hadn't been fired up to terrify. It wasn't too terrifying – for us – at the time, the ram-raid on the Olds' camp. Mostly, it was just – easy. Easy as falling off a log. It was all going down the way we planned it. Picking over the Olds' camp would be sweet as picking deer-fat off the bone.

One thing wasn't so sweet. Windmilling down the ridge ahead of the others, it had to be *me* that fronted the war-hero face-to-face.

He didn't look too sweet at all when he burst out of a shattered bender right in front of me with wild eyes and hair and spittle all over his beard whenever he roared. And did he ever roar. He almost – not quite – grabbed me in passing, but I slipped away like a fish, then feinted a rush to see what he was made of. I'll never know why, since I was all front and bloodrush myself. *Not* a good idea. The chapped old war-hero stood his ground and roared so I'd never forget what he was made of – or what I was, either.

"I'll tan your hides! Hooligans! Vandals! Thieves! Let me get my hands on 'em! I'll give 'em a taste of what they're missing!"

He lifted a digging stick and whirled it. He looked so brave and so pathetic both at the same time that I wondered – for a moment – what I was doing. Then the moment passed. Lots of moments passed in a headstrong rush of ripping, smacking and stealing.

After the raid was over we all went back to the sandpits and got pretty stupid on (stolen) pine-nut gin. I quickly drank the old war-hero out of my mind, plus any injured Olds. So they weren't *all* out of camp that morning on some senior citizens' smoked-fish fest, like our top scouts reported they'd be. Tough, if you didn't like kippers. What was that to the Pits?

I guess you're surprised I changed sides. Not as surprised as I was, that first morning I woke up under the dunes and remembered I belonged to the Pits. Then it all flooded back. Argos. The amber bear. Grub Finger's hand closing over my arm like a claw. The distant look in Argos' eyes that told me I was killing him. At that moment I knew I'd never be any better than I was then. I might as well be where I belonged. *The Pits*. With that rag-bag of washed-up losers out on the dunes. Once you hit bottom, there's no place else to go. I felt relieved about that. Once you *know* you're the pits, you can do anything you like.

Take pillaging – we called it grazing. Nothing to it, once you don't care what you do. Ram-raiding the Olds' camp was the most fun I'd had in a long time. We knew what we had to do. The thing was, psyching ourselves up to *do* it. With zero self-respect, I had a head start on the rest – except, maybe, Grub Fingers. Grub Fingers'd given us a few pointers – the best way to come up on 'em, what was worth lifting, what wasn't. Grub Fingers, like Ma, was in it for all he could get. We all were. Looking after Number One was as natural as breathing in the Pits. There wasn't even a price to pay. Except, sometimes, at night.

I said, "Don't they ever come to you in your sleep? They do me."

Grub Fingers scowled. "Who?"

"The Olds. All the people you robbed. Sometimes I dream they're hurt and I care. Or sometimes they crowd round and judge me."

"Eat any mussels before you bunk down?"

"Yeah," I nodded. "Sometimes."

"That'll do it. Don't eat no mussels. Sleep by the stream. That way you don't get no stick."

What he meant was my bad dreams were down to eating shellfish. Only I knew they weren't. I still had a conscience. Somewhere.

Grub Fingers was a puzzle. He never drank. He never chewed gum. He oiled his topknot daily. Anti-booze and anti-gum, "clean" in his habits by Pits' standards, Grub Fingers was one of the most disgusting individuals I'd ever met, and almost – very nearly – the lowest of the low. I knew for a fact he sold his own grandmother. At fifty-four she was still going strong, yet she'd made, he complained, only five lousy hides on the packhorse market, some nine or ten years previously. Can you believe that. Five lousy hides. Grub snorted. Prices had doubled – trebled – since he'd traded his grandmother in. Grub Fingers still saw his grandmother now and again. She'd pass through every few months or so with some burden or other, loudly cursing her fate. Usually Ma Fingers took her a scoopful of water. She was never very grateful.

It was Grub Fingers who'd stood sponsor for me in the Pits' camp, that first painful evening I learned not to care about anything. The evening after the afternoon I lost Argos' trust for ever. I could think about that now. It didn't hurt a bit.

It turned out Grub Fingers had had his eye on the Pits versus Axes scene for quite a while. Grub went in for kidnapping. The fact that we ran into each other – literally – was a bit of a bonus for Grub. I wouldn't fetch a ransom. But there was always a chance I might be useful. He didn't have to twist my arm. I followed him willingly to the sandpits. After the look Argos gave me, I'd've followed Grub over a cliff. The Axes? They're pathetic, I told the Pits, ditching any last remaining shreds of self-respect. On the nod from Grub, Limpets had skipped the Hazing and let me in. Pity you can't see the ghost of the Horde mark they gave me with a spot of boiling pitch. That was the (only) brave part. The only part of the whole thing I can actually look back on without wincing.

I still saw the family now and again. I knew Argos would look after them – love them, in time, with luck. Sometimes I hid in the reeds and watched them loving him back. Sometimes Bee wanted to slap his chest. Most times he'd let her, laughing. He made a pretty good dad. Plus, he bound up my mother's leg better'n I ever used to. As well as being superdad, Argos tried to win me back in the beginning. "Come back," he'd whisper, in the shadow of the dunes. "Please. Broddy. Your mum, she's breaking her heart, you know what I mean?"

If only. My mother spat at the mention of my name, I knew that for a fact because I'd watched her. Sometimes I saw Hayta. Hayta looked at me wonderingly: Why? I stared him out: *You don't want to know. Because.*

Now the wind was getting hard-edged at night, with a hint of frost in the air. My sisters would be toasting their toes over Argos' good camp-fire, evenings. But I didn't care about that. I didn't have to be a part of it. Just so they all had each other. I always felt like I was on the outside looking in, even when I was one of the family. Now I really *was* on the outside, I didn't feel any different. Maybe I was a born outsider. Maybe I was a lot more like my dad than I realized.

Things were pretty tense between the Pits and the Axes, at the time I'm thinking about. Messages came and went. The Trial by Force of Hand in the Open had been fixed for fish-net-tightening day-week. Usually fish-net-tightening day – when fishing nets were mended – was a day of rest for almost everyone. But this time next week would see a Cruel and Extraordinary Ordeal by Strength and Endurance. That's how Treak was billing it. He was acting pretty jumpy. No one had crossed his boundaries yet. He aimed to keep it that way.

Arf spied on the Axes for us. We knew he spied both ways. We knew Gargas was spying on Arf, spying on us. Time and again, I glimpsed Gargas hiding in the dunes. Certain he was invisible, Gargas was the world's worst spy. Arf came and went easily between both camps and no one took much notice. Eels made a point of knowing what was really going down. The Axes had held a *major* rally after we trashed the Old's camp. No surprises there. They mustered fifteen, maybe sixteen serious contenders, plus fringe wimps like Arf and some nine-year-olds. It was pretty pathetic, really. We could've taken them down any time we wanted. Which made what happened next all the more surprising.

It was mid-morning, with a sea-breeze lifting ends and corners of rubbish around the camp-site. A stinking mess of feathers, once a seagull, fluttered on the dunes. Arf's cold porridge set grimly in the cookpot. It felt good to be back in the sandpits. All things considered, I didn't regret a thing. That's what I told myself, anyway. Everything that made the sandpits worth fighting for came lazily to mind whenever I thought about the crowded, comfortless platform. Gorging on freshwater shrimps in the sea-outlet stream that tumbled them plumply into your hand whenever you wanted, it was hard to remember why the Axes had ever taken the sandpits for granted. Now they'd lost them. Tough.

Viger Wildgoose wasn't exactly making my heart bleed with his life-story, but I let him spill it anyway. What did I care? The sun beat down with that first-of-autumn feel that only made you want its warmth all the more, for knowing it would soon be gone. This far north, even the friendly Pre-Boreal sun had a way of slipping way down under the cloudline before anyone was ready for winter's cold surprises – like chilblains, ice-locked canoes and tent-hide stiff with hoar-frost.

"When I was born I was very young, didn't know nothing—"

"When you were born you were very young?" I interrupted Viger.

"Yeah." Viger Wildgoose stared at me blankly. "What's so wrong with that?"

"Think about it. How could you *not* be very young?"

"Oh. Yeah. Well." Viger Wildgoose coloured. He didn't like to feel stupid. "Then my mum run off."

"Your mother ran off?" I felt a sudden urge never to interrupt him again in my life. "So what about the family?"

Viger Wildgoose shrugged. "Didn't have no family after that."

I ripped the face and tail off a shrimp. It tasted really good. "So how did you make out on your own? How old were you when this happened?"

Viger Wildgoose pushed back his hair. Then he squared his face in front of mine. "How old d'you think I am now? Go on. How many summers I got?"

This was a poser. I thought of a number, then changed it. Finally I tried to think what age he might want me to *think* he was, then added a year for safety.

"I dunno. Sixteen?"

"Think so?" Viger Wildgoose nodded so long in his thoughts, I caught and ate three plump-tailed shrimps before he joined me – cracking, tearing, munching, matching me shrimp for shrimp. Soon a pinkish pile of body-parts built up between us. It was funny the way the shrimps wore their skeletons on the outside. Viger Wildgoose wore his defences on the outside, too. He wasn't nearly as stupid as he pretended. Watching him eating, I knew he hadn't the faintest idea how old he was. It wasn't so unusual. Not too many people did.

"So," I took up, "why did you – the Pits, I mean – why'd you all come here in the first place?"

"Good grazing." Viger Wildgoose fingered the heavy torque, or twisted necklace, he'd scored in the raid on the Olds' camp. "You know how it is. You reach a prime site. Spread a few rumours. Death and destruction, that kind of thing. Hopefully scare folk off. Sometimes they panic and leave a lot more than they meant to." He grinned. "Plus, we rattled the Axes' cage."

I nodded. "They're some worried you got the sandpits. They're worried what you're going to want next."

"They should be. We walk where we want to. We take what we want."

"Ever walked over the mountain?"

Viger considered Climbing Sky. The mountain's south-facing snow-fields glittered coldly in the sunshine. In the clear morning air it almost felt like you could touch them. The ridge under the summit wore a plume of snow trailing away in a speedwell-blue sky, like the whitest snow-goose feather. It looked like a calm day in heaven up there, but I knew the wind would be shrieking. The wind on Climbing Sky talked in many tongues. Whistling under overhangs, groaning in chimneys and crevasses, it was filled, some said, with spirits. I'd been close enough myself to hear its voice. If you weren't mad or dying when you started over the mountain, it surely wasn't long before you were.

Viger Wildgoose licked his lips. "I tell you, I wouldn't mind trying."

"Think anyone could make it?"

"I know a way."

"You know how to cross the mountain?"

"With your heart," said Viger softly, Climbing Sky mirrored in his eyes. "You cross the mountain with your heart. That's what Horl Stendevenger told me."

"When you know which way to go," I suggested, after a pause.

Viger nodded. "Horl Stendevenger showed me. Over the ridge there, see?"

"What ridge? Where?" I shaded my eyes, searching Climbing Sky's unfriendly face.

"The ridge at the top. The dark place under the ice-shelf?" Viger pointed. "I know there's a way there somewhere."

"So who's Horl Stendevenger?"

"You never heard of Horl Stendevenger? He's only the best deer-hunter *ever*. Only the best thrower on the *whole coast* who ever—"

"Save it. Argos is."

"Yeah?" Viger Wildgoose curled his lip.

"What'd Argos do?"

"Argos threw eighty-nine metres. *Into the same mark twice.*"

"OK. Horl Stendevenger stuck a raging elk *here*?" Viger Wildgoose smacked his forehead. "One spear. Stone dead. Fifty paces."

"Least he could *see* it. Argos took out the Killer Pike of the Lake through three metres of slime after it ate a dog once. Know what? When it finally hauled out, that spear was *dead centre* through its eye, and Argos never even saw it properly. That's throwing."

"Or luck."

"Whichever."

We glared hotly at one another. I felt like beating him in. Then I remembered. I didn't care about anything. Just as well, considering the Axes' next move.

Surprise, surprise. They came swinging through camp like they owned it. It was lucky for them the main party – including Eels and Cud – were away. Except for a few deadbeats moaning in the dunes, the sandpits were virtually deserted. Perhaps they were banking on that. Even so, it took a fair bit of bottle. Vert and Gargas and Gargas' sister and brother; *and my own sister Broddha*; and a twelve-year old pimple called Dug – all under the Leaderene, swinging loosely through the sandpits, knocking everything over. Just like the raid on the Olds, I thought. Only this time the damage was ours.

"Hey," I said. "*Leave it, OK?*"

The Leaderene paused with her knife in our only drinking bladder. Looking at me, smiling, she ripped the knife all the way down the bladder so the water gushed out and boiled in the sand underneath. The empty bladder dripped sadly, turning very slightly one way, then the other. It didn't matter a whole lot. The stream was so near you could spit in it. All the same, did she have to?

I said, "OK. You made your point."

The Leaderene wiped her knife coolly. "Didn't know pigs' bottoms could talk."

"This pig's bottom does." Vert raised his eyebrows. "It thinks it's a person. Look. It walks, it talks, it—"

My sister walked up and kicked me. It really, really hurt – not least because it was just about the first and only contact I'd had with her in weeks. "Go home. Idiot." I pushed her. Hard. "What is this, a game? Go home. You'll get hurt."

"I hope. Then Argos'll come out an' *kill* you." She hated me. I couldn't really blame her.

Viger Wildgoose got up. He spat a plug of birch gum into the sand. Then he kicked the hearth to pieces – slowly, deliberately, sending up clouds of fine-grained charcoal dust. He looked up through charcoal-dust hair. "Find anything else to rubbish, be my guest." He smiled crookedly. "We got nothing to lose, see? That's the difference between us. Mind if I clean my spear?"

Drawing his spear lightly across Gargas' chest,

Viger Wildgoose made a show of cleaning it. Gargas' eyes flashed dangerously. Gargas was mad as a cat at the best of times. I had a feeling things could easily get out of hand. Someone – not me – might be sorry.

"What's this about?" I fronted. "So I changed Hordes. So what? Can't we just live with that?"

"You'd like that, wouldn't you?" The Leaderene put her face in mine. Her black eyes drilled right through me. "What about what you did to the Olds?"

"What *about* the Olds? It was a laugh, right? No one got hurt. Just scared."

"That makes it all right then, does it?"

"Wasn't me anyway," I lied. "I never did much."

"But you would've, if you could've?"

"Maybe." I shrugged. "Take a hike, why don't you? Get out before the others come. You better watch your back."

"You're telling *me* to watch *my* back? In *our* camp in the sandpits?"

"Ours now. You lost it."

"No," said the Leaderene softly. "No. *You* lost it this time, Broddy."

"It's like this." Vert broke the too-long pause that followed. "We just came to say, have a nice day."

Grinning, Vert upended our one and only cookpot. The grim-looking barley-meal porridge Arf had made earlier plopped out on the sand. It wasn't much, but it might have been dinner. Vert messed the porridge with his foot. Then he looked up. "Enjoy."

Gargas took the empty cookpot – his mother's empty cookpot – with a grunt of recognition. "Hope you choke on it," he added.

"Choke on it while you *can*," the Leaderene threw over her shoulder – backing off, as always, with exquisite timing. "You won't be here much longer."

"We'll see about that." Viger Wildgoose sneered. "Next fish-net-tightening day."

We watched them disappear over the dunes – my sister, I noticed, last. I wondered if my mother knew she was hanging out with the Axes. I pictured my mother's face. But I didn't want to think about that. The strife over the sandpits had already taken the Axes, I could see, quite a bit further than anyone really wanted to go. The Cruel and Extraordinary Contest next fish-net-tightening day should settle it once and for all. But I didn't want to think about that either. I got up to go, dredging my brains for a lie. I needn't have bothered. Viger had one himself.

"You know all that stuff about my mother running off and how I never had a family an' stuff?"

"Yeah," I said, guardedly. "What?"

"I made it all up."

"You made it up? Why?"

"It wasn't that way at all. My dad used to hit me. He really got stuck into me, once. Then I ran away. Been on my own ever since."

I searched his eyes. "You making this up as well?"

Viger Wildgoose shrugged. Then he set off towards the beach, probably limpet-picking. Old Viger was big on limpets. Limpets. I thought about my mother again. Some things you can't dodge for ever.

I watched Viger Wildgoose crossing the dunes in his blundering, straight-as-the-crow-flies way, scaring the wildlife for miles. He would never be a friend. He would never let me, or anyone else, close enough for that. No one had friends, in the Pits. Freedom meant being answerable to no one and nothing, caring about no one and nothing, not even family. No one in the sandpits could count on anything, or anyone, except themselves. For the moment, I liked it that way.

9

The Shell Midden – Naal's Revenge – Understanding Arf

I found my mother cracking limpets in the midden. I guessed she'd be in the midden around mid-day. She was busy with her back to me in a mess of whelks and oysters. A slithering stack of oily-looking mussels spilled around her, all gathered along the coastline, a half-hour's walk across the dunes. I could see the flies were bothering her. The shell middens, or rubbish holes, in the gravel beds were always thick with flies. Where there weren't flies, there were gulls. The broken, smelly shells attracted gulls – one reason we buried the shells in middens. One reason the women did, anyway.

I checked the scene carefully. No one else around. Way in the river-fed sumps behind my mother's head, the swamp willows wagged in the distance. I didn't look inland. That way lay the cookpit. Rest in peace, I thought, Dad. You don't have a lot of choice.

The lake lapped lightly on the gravel-beds. They

acted a bit like a filter. Here the water was good for washing, scouring, rinsing. The tan-coloured flint-gravel wasn't a whole lot of good for anything else. The odd workable flint from the gravel beds might make an easy tent-post hammer, nothing too important. Dog-flint, they called it – good for throwing at dogs, and not much else. If you wanted medium-grade flint for something slightly better, you had to smash-and-wedge it from the well-used outcrop beyond the pine woods. For state-of-the-art, weapons-grade core-flint you had to visit the flint mines and trade your heart out, shouting the way the women did trading shellfish.

Every two or three days or so, the women gathered shellfish. I watched my mother expertly crack and open limpet shells with her hammer, shaking the liquid-fleshed animals into her basket. The other women had taken their grass-lined baskets to the lake. Their laughter lifted over on the wind, making me feel sorry – more sorry than I was already – for my mother. My mother's poisoned leg made her slow. I watched her a long time. I hadn't known *how* slow.

She glanced up briefly as I joined her. "Here," I said, "let me help you."

My mother paused, her limpet hammer in mid-air. Then she gave me her hard face. "Help me. You can't even help yourself."

She worked quickly, bitterly, as though I weren't there. It wasn't a promising start. I stacked her a pile of shellfish beside her cracking stone, so she didn't have to reach. Then I fussed the mussels into a (more untidy) heap. They skated over one another, no matter what you did. They just weren't tidy molluscs. Their worm-cast, glossy, blue-black shells fascinated me. I looked up. My mother had something to say.

"I hope you'll stop this nonsense over the sand-pits after this Contest." She pursed her lips after "Contest", like she was sorry she'd let anything slip at all.

"Sure." I smiled awkwardly. "That's the whole point."

"I'm serious." She looked up. "I really want you to, Broddy. I haven't – I haven't much time."

"What d'you mean, you haven't much time?"

"I'm only glad we've got Argos. That man's a gift from Naal. I've taken religion, Broddy. I might be going over."

"Over the ridge to the Olds?" I searched my mother's eyes.

"Maybe. My leg, it's – bad. Better the girls don't see."

"You're not going over. Not for a long time yet." I swallowed hugely. This was my mother. Telling me she might be going to die. "Anyway. Argos won't let you."

My mother softened. "What would we do without him?"

"Have someone like my dad again." It came out bitterly, before I could stop it. All the distance I'd halved between us flooded back, and all the anger with it. "I'm not coming home. If the Pits lose the Contest, I'm leaving."

"Thanks for letting me know," my mother said flatly. "Pass me the mussel scoop, will you?"

I passed her the beaver-skull scoop. Digging it into the mussel heap, my mother charged her cracking stone with sliding, blue-black shells. Then she took up her hammer. Her blows were vicious, sharp, regular. She didn't look up again.

I swept a pile of limpet shells into the midden for her. They showered down like an icefall on the pearly-grey pile almost filling the hole. The stink of rotten shellfish wafted up. Soon it would be time to dig another midden. I got up to go. There didn't seem much else to say. Just before I reached the treeline, I turned. My mother was standing slowly; so slowly, so painfully, every angle her body made hurt me somewhere inside. This – I thought – *this* is what I'm turning my back on. Not my mother. Only the feeling that I need her. It's what she did herself, when she left my grandmother. It's what she'd want me to do. Isn't it?

"Mum!" I yelled. "I'll send you stuff! Promise! I'll send you pelts, when I got 'em!"

I don't know whether she heard me or not. I like to think she did. Anyway, I reasoned, all the way to Treak's, they were better off without me. Argos would provide for the family miles better'n I ever could, that was for sure. It was almost certainly true. But somehow, I didn't feel better.

* * *

"I want some devilment," I told Treak. "Something really strong."

The Bedeviller looked surprised when I greeted him. I had the feeling I'd caught him on the hop.

"Broddy Brodson. How's it hanging?"

"Good. Not really. Bad, in fact."

The way I saw it, Ma Fingers had to be stopped. Stopping Ma Fingers would be the last truly selfless thing I'd do. A real and major threat to the Tribe of Families, Ma Fingers would sell the platform and everyone on it down the river, the moment the men set out on a three-day hunt. The moment the platform was undefended, she'd give the nod to Eels. I wasn't supposed to care, but I did. It would be *my* family we were robbing. My mother. My sisters. My home. I wasn't – perfectly – the pits yet. I told myself I'd save the platform for old times' sake. Then after, I'd be reborn under hard and ruthless gods, gods not even Arf would recognize. Soon I'd be perfectly selfish. Then nothing would hurt me ever again, not even the memory of Dad. Wasn't that, after all, the payoff?

"Who's behind the screen?" I asked. The feet underneath were a giveaway.

Treak rubbed his nose. "Guess you been rumbled. Come on out, Norbert," he said.

The birch-wattle screen shook slightly. Norbert Arthagarth Haagerbarta appeared beside it. How many strange disguises, how many unlikely locations, would Arf pop up in next? Of course his name was Norbert. He'd been Arf so long, I'd forgotten.

"Hi. I just – hi." Arf grinned. It figured. Strangely two of a kind, I saw Arf and Treak had deep and mysterious business. It looked like Treak had a helper. Arf had sorcerer's apprentice written all over him.

"Anyway." I stuck to the business in hand with an effort. "The thing is, I want a potion against Ma Fingers. A real goer."

Treak seemed to relax. Maybe he was jumpy because he'd grassed me up to Argos about the amber bear, it occurred to me suddenly. What was he, scared? In his wildest dreams – afraid of *me*? I looked at the Bedeviller. For all his voodoo, what was he? A little old man in a hat.

"So, so, so." Treak narrowed his eyes, flitting glances along his shelves of potions made of repellent bits of animals. "Do we want fatal, or not?"

"Not. Disabling'll do. I want her out of action."

Treak chuckled and clucked along his shelves. At last he settled on something. Uncorking an ibex horn, he took a deep and luxurious sniff. "Oh, yeah." He sniffed again, enjoying. "Hoo! Yeah. That's the one." He handed it over. "Mind how you go with that stuff."

I looked in the antelope horn. The oily-looking liquid inside it niffed like a thousand oysters. "What will it do?"

"Twist her bowels."

"Horribly?"

Treak clutched his guts, miming terminal illness. He sucked in his cheeks, crossed his eyes and legs. Arf cracked up in the corner. Treak grinned through gum-stained teeth, glancing at Arf, enjoying himself. "A month in the bushes. Guaranteed."

"That'll do nicely." I grinned at him back.

A month in the bushes would just about do it. Call it Naal's Revenge. Paying Treak with shellfish, I noticed his seer's bowl of water. "Been casting the future again?" I asked, not really wanting to know.

"*I* have," volunteered Arf. "I got flair, I have."

Treak moved closer. "Sees more'n I ever did," he confided, radiating smells. "He sees all sorts. Got a real flair for second-sight, that boy."

"Sees who's going to win the Contest, does he?" I moved away slightly. It was that or fall down.

"He has visions." Treak moved closer still. "He sees the mountain. He sees *beyond* the mountain. He sees everything."

"Lots of important people're going to come and see me, they are," announced Arf self-consciously. "I'm going to be famous, one day."

"That right?"

Arf nodded. Then he said: "I'm thinking of calling myself Norbert the Befriender. What d'you think?"

"Yes, Arf," I said. "Sounds great." Treak's natural successor grinned. He'd look good in ritual bearskin, I decided. Norbert the Befriender. I could see it all. "Sounds great, Arf," I told him.

Treak stopped me outside the tent. "Wait up. There's something – I didn't mean no harm."

"You mean the amber bear?"

The Bedeviller nodded, his eyes shifting, calculating the advantage in keeping me sweet.

"Forget it." I shrugged. "Things happen."

I turned to go.

"Then there's boy Vertigern."

I turned. "Vert's been here? What about him?"

"Boy Vertigern got some heavy three-minute poison. For the Axes, although he don't say so. I tell you, you want to watch out."

"Thanks, Treak," I told him, going.

He wasn't a bad old stick. Maybe I'd save him from Eels, after all. The little old man in the hat might, after all, be useful. So might a dunk in the river. I changed course inland a little, walking briskly, leaving the swamplands at last for the rushing, choppy race of the cool-breathed, rock-scrambled river.

On my way I found Ur. I don't know what took a hold of me, but something told me I could do it. I came up behind him. Ur looked around incuriously. He knew it was me. Something filled my chest like it would burst. Running lightly over the water-meadow, I vaulted onto Ur's back. A tremor ran through both of us. Ur thought about it. Then he took off like a whirlwind, plunging and threshing through the riverside mallows, bellowing panic for the both of us. I'll never forget that wild ride, or the feeling I had when I stole it. Clamping my

105

legs against his tar-black sides, ducking front-end madness and back-end murder – Ur's scything horns and the switching tonnage behind – I must've stayed on Ur's back all of a count of fifty-fishes-over-the-weir before he jack-knifed me off. I laughed my head off after he ditched me. Ur crashed off, bellowing, through the reed-beds. I'd never tried to ride him before. He'd probably never forgive me.

When I finally reached the sort of drowsing, mood-filled backwater that I really needed to bathe in, I found myself staring at my reflection instead. Was it really me? No wonder Treak seemed nervous. I looked like the devil-troll from hell. Looking at the wasted, mud and blood-streaked face in the pool, I felt a bit nervous, myself. I hardly recognized what I'd become. Every mother's nightmare. I looked the part, I really did. Rebel without remorse.

Smiling – I couldn't stop – I dived from Arf's dancing platform. The deep, dark, ice-cold water cut me like a knife. I was better – more deeply myself, more perfect – than I'd ever been before.

10

Return of Imchat – The Contest – An Appeal

Malice, dorkiness, ambition. Fish-net-tightening day dawned bright and crisp and chilly. Arf's wild-barley porridge had been especially thick that morning. Interrupted by the Voice of Imchat while soaking antlers under the waterfall, Arf told me he'd had a vision that today was a day of destiny.

"What did she say?" I asked guardedly.

Arf put on a dream-like tone, "*Dreadful Imchat Anoints the Chosen One.*"

"Chosen for what?"

Arf looked mysterious. "The Anointed of Imchat will keep his own counsel."

"Arf," I began, "don't you realize they're using you? Don't you realize it's only—"

Arf got up like someone pulled his string. "Sorry. Gotta go."

"Catch you later." I watched him disappear over the dunes, swallowed in minutes by a fresh-faced mist off the sea. The sun had only just risen.

Preparing, with the others, to give the Axes – and anyone else attending the Ordeal by Strength and Endurance that day – a real treat, I was prepared, with the others, to pull out all the stops. There were some occasions you needed full battle drag plus warpaint. This was one of them.

Everyone was painting up. Eels made a line of white spots along her arms. Her partner not-Eels – name of Burin – held still for a whorl of red-ochre, mid-forehead. I crushed a little chalk dust in a shell. Then I crumbled some ochre. Might as well go to town. Give them all a thrill. Then I had a better idea. Ditching the paint, I kicked up the fireplace a bit. Charcoal-black, why not?

The Contest had been fixed for midday. The sun was high over Climbing Sky before we were up and ready. Eels put on her stolen drum. Viger Wildgoose gave the sign. Eels hit the skins and drummed us out in style. We solemnly circled the lake, striking left for the flint mines via the Olds' ridge. The Olds freaked out when they saw us. Several followed on at a safe distance, keen to see the Pits brought low (they wished) by the Axes. Trial by Force of Hand in the Open was a serious matter. What kind of Contest would it be? We may as well turn to Needcliff:

Why are some skulls thicker than others? Perhaps because they originate from areas where conflicts are traditionally resolved by blows to the head. In ritual contests of this sort, two people strike each other in turn with their (wooden) dig-

ging sticks, a victor being declared when one of them can no longer rise.

So now you know. Two people strike each other in turn with their wooden digging sticks. Simps goes on:

As many as 57 per cent of all skulls in the study community bore depressed fractures. The presence of similar fractures on aboriginal skeletons more than 11,000 years old shows that the practice is of ancient origin and may have been widespread.

You bet it was. (I'm quoting freely from the Nerdcliff blockbuster *The Deer Hunters: Magic and Ritual in Pre-Boreal Society*. I notice Simps has three copies of each of his own books on the office shelves. I think that says a lot.)

Back to the Contest. I always felt it should've been called Trial by Force of Head. No prizes for guessing who the Axes' champion was. In four generations, reckoned Arf's toothless mother, no one had had a thicker skull than her eldest and only son. You got it. The Axes were fielding Arf.

The moment we reached the assignation site I saw the Axes were up for it. Coolly shouldering ritual axes, they were making quite an impression on the crowd gathering around them. The raised mounds of the flint mine diggings made an ideal arena for a contest. Everyone could see. Everyone could share in the winner's triumph. The colourful-looking crowd was in holiday mood. Everyone who wasn't tightening their fishing-nets was there. I looked around. The Axes' champion – the

Chosen One – looked more than a little green. The Anointed of Imchat knew he was in for a hammering, with little choice one way or the other. The Leaderene stood behind him, feathered to the eyebrows with sleek-looking crows' wings. They matched her flashing eyes. Poor old Arf had been leaned on pretty heavily. He clearly thought awesome Imchat would strike him dead if he failed.

We looked pretty awesome ourselves, that fishnet-tightening day. Bristling with spears, beaded and patterned and henna'd, mud-plastered and stiffly quilled with feathers, streaked and barred and spotted, red-ochred to the hilt, the Pits were more than ready to join battle over the sandpits. We crossed the arena to the sound of Eels' drum. The effect was pretty dramatic. Viger Wildgoose rattled his spirit-shaker ferociously as he led the way up the mound. A dead gull hung from his belt, its broken neck wagging as he walked. Almost everyone had made an effort to look bizarre. Whelp – the intellectually challenged – had threaded an awl, or needle, of elk-bone through both cheeks. It always looked impressive. Whelp had holes in both cheeks, anyway. He often kebabbed himself for a laugh. I had on my worst-best pelt, a disreputable-looking beaver. Also, I'd rolled in charcoal. Might as well be the dark man – *Brod* – with a vengeance. It made me look like the cave-bear from hell. I rolled my eyes as I walked, giving the crowd my mad look. Cud made the death-hoot behind. I liked the way the crowd fell back as we passed. It made me feel good, really good, as we took the field.

"Good turnout. Guess they'll just about know what's what, after we trash the Axes," blustered the boy Spider. "They jus' about better watch themselves, is all."

He adjusted the thick leather plate on his chest. My little sister could've ripped it off and blown Spider away before breakfast. He was far more pathetic than he knew. Almost everyone was, except Viger. Viger was standing as champion, I supposed. I turned to check with Cud. It was hard to bring myself down to Cud's level. Literally.

"Know who's doing the honours?"

"Yeah," said Cud, "don't you?"

"No." I gave him a double-take. "What?"

Cud smiled unpleasantly. "You are, aren't you?"

"Me? I got a head like an egg. I couldn't even—"

"Relax," said Cud. "It's Eels."

Eels it was. Dressed savagely and exclusively in baby animal pelts, she wore the kind of look that didn't encourage conversation. I didn't exactly feel I could ask her how she felt. How would *you* feel, with a thorough-going public head-licking ahead of you? There were worse things in life, I supposed. One of them was, I saw Argos. Argos' eyes slid over me like I was a tree or a rock or something. It hurt a whole lot more than anything he or anyone else might've said. I tried not to mind, but I did. I wasn't perfect yet.

111

Treak stepped out in voodoo drag, his hat alive with curses. Scored on papery pigs' gut, the symbols streamed on the wind as Treak consecrated a circle for the Contest with the full picnic of endless sacred pledges to all the spirits of chance and fortune who happened to be listening, and most of those who weren't. Everyone waited. Eels' hair lifted very slightly on the breeze. The Leaderene's crow feathers rippled. Someone dropped a spear. Treak droned on. Would he never stop? At last he brought out the ochre in a nifty ritual pot. When Treak had finally drawn the circle in red ochre, the Contest could begin.

"Ladees and gentlemen." Argos had taken up a commanding position where two flint-diggings met. "Ladees and gentlemen, we bring you a Trial of Strength and Endurance, a knockout Contest of unlimited duration. On my left hand, representing the Pits, Elin 'Eels' Rainmaker – a big hand for the challenger."

We all roared and stamped. Eels coolly acknowledged the crowd, raising both arms, showing off her baby animal skins, fluffy tummy side out.

"And on my right hand, out of the Tribe of Families, representing home Horde the Axes, I give you Norbert 'Stonehead' Haagerbarta!"

The Axes howled. The Pits whistled and hooted. Arf acknowledged all of it with a silly great smile on his face. Was it possible he didn't realize what he was up for? Or did all the attention make up for it?

On the nod from Argos, Eels and Arf took up opposite sides of the circle. Full respect to Eels. No one could've been cooler. It was obvious she'd been soaking her head. I wondered what she'd used. Fermented birch-sap was supposed to harden the scalp best, but the yellow tidemark over her ears told me she may've used oak tannin.

Final bets were lodged with Falco Fingers, every gambler's nightmare, since he hardly ever paid out. Everyone talked amongst themselves. I scored a couple of packs of salted pine-nuts off the pimple Dug, promising to pay him later. But Duggie dug his heels in, insisting he didn't give credit. The pathetic-looking slave to the Axes pretty soon scurried off with his tray of nuts, once I opened the packs with my knife. My biggest hafted dagger.

Argos announced the Rules of the Contest in a big voice. Blows to be exchanged alternately. No second attempt in the event of a miss. No ducking. No moving out of the way. Parrying blows with an arm is acceptable under the rules. A winner will be declared when one party can no longer rise, or when one party concedes. *Winner takes the sand-pits unopposed.* He addressed the champions: "You know what I want. A good, clean contest. Respect your opponent. Play by the rules." Then he examined the digging sticks before they were handed out.

OK. The wooden digging sticks – you can still see ones very like them today, wrongly catalogued as paddles by J.S. Needcliff, in the Arturo-Chapman Museum, display case 201 – the wooden digging sticks used in contests like this are the kind of blunt object you'd have quite a bit of trouble actually hurting someone with. They're made of the kind of spongy wood that soaks up anything you throw at it. Also, they're not very heavy. Deliberately. It made contests so much more interesting, the longer they went on. Technique was everything. Brute force only made the eyes water. The trick was to stun your opponent with a blow in just the right place.

Arf had taken the first crack to his scalp by the time I finished my pine-nuts. Hoo! The crowd took it lightly enough – lighter than Arf, anyway. Climbing to his feet, Arf gripped his digging stick. Eels was looking good. After Arf cracked her over the head – hoo! – she was still looking good. Not quite as good as before, perhaps, but the old scalp was holding up well. Not that Arf's wasn't. Eels took careful aim this time. Wait for it – crack! Arf blinked. He blanched slightly, dropping to one knee. Then he got up slowly.

"Finish it, Haagerbarta," the Leaderene ordered coldly.

Norbert Haagerbarta tried to. The crowd held its breath. Arf aimed, struck – *and missed*. Everyone roared. Advantage Pits.

Eels raised her digging stick. She licked her lips. She looked at Arf. Smiling very slightly, she fetched Arf a monumental crack across the cranium. The sound of Eels' digging stick connecting with Arf's skull popped around the circle, setting everyone's teeth on edge. Nothing happened for a moment or two. Norbert "Stonehead" Haagerbarta swayed very slightly. Then he fell down. Eels made a victory dance. The crowd loved her. Just at that moment, I think I did, too. Argos started counting. Arf moaned and staggered, getting up on "ten".

"Imchat expects," hissed the Leaderene – rather unfairly, I thought – "Imchat expects those who are worthy to *win*."

Eels offered her head again. Argos handed Arf his digging stick. Arf examined it carefully as though he'd never seen it before in his life, until Argos told him "ready". Arf gathered himself. The faces all around him didn't help. What were they, ghost-devils? Ancestors? Maybe the Ghost Chant would help.

"Stop that singing or I'll hit you myself." The Leaderene put a foot in the circle.

"Seconds out," ordered Argos. "*If* you don't mind. Thank you."

Arf looked lop-sidedly at Eels. For some reason, he had to hit her on the head. It seemed a pity. She looked rather nice. He'd rather just lie down and think about it. He looked around. They were all rather nice, his friends, his family, his Tribe. Shame it all had to end. Shame the centuries had to fall down on top of them all, and the snows had to cover them up. There was no escape. Everyone here would be dust and dead and buried. Suddenly Arf was crying.

"*Cliffson!*" blurted Arf. "*Nee-cliff! Dad! He's over here! Sorry, iceman! Annamay! Annamay Nee-cliff, don't!*"

"What's up with *him*, like I care?" Cud asked.

"He sees the future." I shrugged. "I think he's prophesying."

"*Poor iceman. Cover him up, poor iceman,*" crooned Arf.

"Ready. Strike!" said Argos.

Still prophesying, Arf brought down his digging-stick on something, anything, that wasn't a part of himself. Eels caught the blow easily on her forearm.

"*Parried!*" ruled Argos. The crowd went wild.

Poor Arf. Eels centred herself. A hush fell. Suddenly Eels jumped up and brought down her stick like a tiger. Arf thought about many things in the moments after she hit him. His expression changed through puzzled to surprised, then back to puzzled again. Then he wilted. The Pits cheered wildly. Argos invited Arf to get up. Arf declined, feeling he'd rather lie down. The Pits stamped and hooted. Argos invited Arf to get up a second, then a third, and final, time. Arf relaxed full-length on the ground. His Second answered for him. He didn't think he would.

Argos declared a winner: "Representing the Pits, the winner by a knockout – and uncontested champion – I give you *Elin 'Eels' Rainmaker*!"

Argos held Eels' hand high. Everyone stamped and cheered for the uncontested champ. Everyone except Arf. The Axes' champion would be fully relaxed for quite a while to come. For what was probably the first time ever, Arf's thick skull had let him down. But not his good nature. Even unconscious, he was smiling.

"Idiot. Loser. Nerd." The Leaderene flipped Arf's arm on his chest with her toe. "Useless, no-hope excuse for a…"

"Hey. He done his best, all right?" Argos pushed her once with his finger. "No abusin' contestants, you know what I mean?"

"I hate a bad loser, don't you?" Cud sneered.

White with fury, the Leaderene whipped out an axe. Argos tripped her up in the moment of lodging it safely in Cud's skull.

"Not here. Not now. Not ever."

"Who says?" The Leaderene simmered.

"Me. I say. Got it?" Argos dropped her arm dismissively.

"No one talks to the Axes that way. Not even Argos the Thrower."

Mortally wounded in the dignity area, the Leaderene huffed off with more than half the Axes. No one noticed them go. The crowd rushed the mound, lifting Eels on their shoulders.

Argos held up his hands for silence. "Following a decision by the judges, the result of the Contest is declared: possession of the sandpits is granted unopposed and without duration to the Horde calling itself – *the Pits!*

The crowd roared its approval. Watched by

Argos, each remaining Axe in turn swore to keep the peace. Our victory was as complete as any could be – so we thought. I made sure I got to the root-beer before it went. We all toasted Eels. Then she toasted herself, drowning her head in root-beer. The crowd finally filtered away. Arf limped off with his helpers. It looked like he'd live to fight another day. After everyone else had cleared off we mucked around with the flint-mine equipment a bit, sending Duggie the pine-nut down a forty-foot pit in a leather bucket. He didn't appreciate it much.

I felt pretty mellow, let me tell you, after my first slug of root-beer since my dad's last – very last – birthday celebration. We all felt mellow after the root-beer. We sat around swapping stories a while. I was hoping someone else knew the one about the three elk under a fig-tree. Thing is, I forgot the punch-line. Three elk under a fig tree. One elk says to the other, Wonder who's eating the figs? Second elk says, Beats me – why don't you try asking *him*? So the first elk says to the third elk, Wonder who's eating the figs? And the third elk looks up and says – fax the Needcliff Laboratory on 770 76088 with the punchline if you have it. (That's not what the third elk says.)

The rubbish-fight started with the apple-peel. It got very silly, very quickly. After I'd had a rotten quince or two in the face plus a whole handful of beech-mast down my back, I was glad when Viger blew up a pig's bladder. We played football until everyone, Eels especially, was just about ready to drop. Then we snuck around to the platform. There wasn't an Axe in sight. Just the usual dreary bunch of deerskin-flayers working the shoreward racks. A few fish-net-tighteners, determined to tie up loose ends. And plenty of holiday food.

Later, much later, after an afternoon's blow-out on top grub like (stolen) snack-roast snout of pig and most of the froth off the mead vat, we were rolling back to camp feeling pretty good all round, when Spider – I thought he went back earlier – windmilled into us shouting panic. He looked pretty funny with sand and mud in his hair. But Spidey wasn't joking. He'd never been more serious in his life.

"Where's Viger? Get Viger! *They only took the camp!*"

"Take it down," burped Whelp. "Who took what, whenever?"

"The camp!" blared Spider, full volume. "They went and took the camp behind our backs!"

Cud woke up. Then Eels. "Who did, the Axes?"

Spider spluttered, unable to get it all out. "I went back to the sandpits, they took 'em while we was out drinking – they got the stream, the shrimp-beds, everything – that piece with the black eyes, she got Viger's hammock – there's guards posted everywhere, like they been there hours – I tell you, I only jus' got out…"

Oh, treachery. She *would* have it all, and then some. The too-ambitious Leaderene had broken

119

the peace already. So much for that. The three-hour-old cease-fire was over before it had really started. Sending Spider on for Viger, we were running sick as parrots back to camp, when all at once I spotted Argos.

Argos was waiting at the crossroads where four sand-streaked paths kissed and parted. Once I saw him – once he saw that I saw him – I had to stop. He had a kid with him. The Beast. Why would Argos wait for me? After all that had gone down before? The root-beer was catching up with me. I could almost swear I saw two Argoses, where one was more than enough. The others flooded on. I watched them go, avoiding Argos' eye, wishing I could join them.

First I felt hard and angry, remembering the way he'd ignored me before the Contest. Then I softened, picking up the mood. There was something deep between us, but I didn't know what it was. The Beast examined her feet. She wasn't about to drop me any clues.

"How's it going?" I managed at last, a million (better) things I might've said hanging unspoken in the air.

"Like you *care*." The Beast clamped her mouth shut like Mum.

"It's like this, Broddy." Argos paused. I noticed he couldn't look me in the eye.

"Like what?"

The Beast's brown eyes threatened to tell me something. Something I didn't want to know.

"Your mum…"

"Mum? What about her?"

"And me, I…" Argos looked desperate. "Broddy, please. It's only me, on me own. Three little girls to look after. Broddy. You got to help me. Your mother went over the ridge."

"She went over the ridge already?"

Argos took a deep breath. "You don't understand. She's dead."

11
Retreat to Mended Vision – Trying Times for All

The Archaeologist's Daughter rang her mother last night. It seemed her mother lived some distance away. She had plenty to say. I only zeroed in on her after some freaky, time-locked dream about Argos. I drift in and out, it's funny. First I'm around, then I'm not. I guess that's being a ghost.

"… and one elk says to the other, Wonder who's eating the figs? So the second elk says, Beats me – why don't you try asking him? So the first elk says to the third elk, Wonder who's eating the figs? And the third elk …"

"Darling. Is there a point to this?" The Archaeologist's Ex sounded more than a little peevish.

"Not really, there isn't a punchline. It's something I found on the office computer. I've been trying to think what the punchline could be, no one's come up with one yet."

"Seen the *Commentator* this morning? Your father's in all the papers. It says – let me see – 'The remains of the man from pre-history discovered last month high on Ben Uther continue to pose a mystery. Where was he going? Why was he there? 'The man we call Uther was probably of Danish stock,' says J.S. Needcliff, team leader at the Institute of Archaeo-Pathology—'"

"Seen it. Not a bad picture, is it? Not a bad picture of Dad, I mean."

"How's the work experience going?"

"Fine. I've been in molecular medicine today. Looking at DNA chains."

"Sounds marvellous."

"We found eight people locally with the same DNA sequence as Fred's – Uther's – the iceman's. *Sixteen* from a sample including Danes and Germans. Shows he was probably Danish, 'cept the mitochondrial record's the same for both…"

"It's all a bit technical for me, I'm afraid. How's Dad?"

"Dad's OK. I'm in the office with him again tomorrow. Collating radio-carbon data, probably."

"It's not all work, I hope. I hope you're going out and having fun. It *is* a holiday, after all."

"It's a bit difficult. I don't really know anyone here, and Dad's a fat lot of use."

"I thought you might spend some time together. Go out and see a few things."

"So did I. I don't think he knows I exist."

"Darling. Don't be sad."

"Try not to."

"Missing you."

"Mm. Missing you. It's amazing to think people probably had the same sort of conversation as this in Fred's – the iceman's time. I'm *not* going to call him Fred."

"I'm not sure I know what you mean."

"Oh, you know, the dad you get isn't always the one you want. That kind of thing."

"Well. I'm sure people have always missed their mothers. I know I missed mine when I left home."

"I'll see you soon. Only a day or two now."

"I'll air your room. Kiss, kiss."

Kiss, kiss, was too much for anyone. The Archaeologist's Daughter made a face. "I'm going to shut the computer down now and get myself a hot chocolate from the machine. It's creepy in the office after everyone's gone home."

"Anna? Make sure you bring all your books home?"

"Will do. 'Bye now. Give you a ring on Tuesday."

The Archaeologist's Daughter killed the phone. Then she turned to the computer. Opening the document titled PITS.DOC, she started wiping the story – my story, Arf's story, her story – *our* story. "Delete document? Are you sure Y or N?" asked the screen. The Archaeologist's Daughter hovered. *Anna Mae Needcliff, don't!*

Perhaps I reached her, who knows? Pausing a while, she finally shrugged, hitting N, then Exit Windows. The computer sighed as she clicked it

124

off. She looked around the office like she could see me or something. Then she put out the lights.

I waited until her footsteps died on distant vinyl tiles. Then I booted up. Every night I enter a little more story on the computer. It helps me make sense of it all. Wondering how a Stone Age illiterate like me knows about reading and writing and computers? I did to start with, too. I started to wonder how I'd "slept" through most of recorded history. How I knew things I never knew before. Then I realized. Not much point entering the Great Beyond if you don't get universal knowledge, right? I'm a ghost, remember? Penetrating everything. Beyond space and time. Reading and writing? No worries.

The first thing I did when I booted up the computer was ghost a spare disk into the machine and copy over the file named PITS.DOC to make the story safe. Why hadn't I backed it up before? I named the copy PITS.BACKUP, burying the disk deep in the academic textbooks under the Nerdcliff desk. Then I opened a new document, calling it PITS.TWO, and wrote up the call I'd just heard. The Archaeologist's Daughter's mother had sounded silly, but warm and concerned and *there*. I remembered everything she'd said. You can't forget, with universal knowledge. One phrase stuck in my mind.

I'm sure people have always missed their mothers. Suddenly the keyboard seems unfriendly, the walls of the office vague. Time and space open out.

125

I'm back on the sand-streaked crossroads with Argos and the Beast, in the moment before he tells me – always the moment *before*, no matter how many times I replay the scene in my mind. Argos opens his mouth. The Beast's brown eyes say it all. Argos takes a deep breath. You don't understand, he says. I play it again, and again. My privilege, being a ghost. I can zap back and forth through time any way I want, and most of the ways I don't.

Sometimes I revisit the shell midden conversation – that's the worst, because there was still time, then, to change things – wondering why I didn't help my mother when I could've. Then I skip to the crossroads again, in the moment before Argos tells me. Argos opens his mouth. He takes a deep breath. You don't understand, he says. You don't understand, she's – I don't hear what he says next, because I rewind the scene yet again. Reliving it won't change a thing, I know. It's about as pointless as a joke without a punchline. The Archaeologist's Ex really hit the nail on the head. It was one of those phrases no one could argue with. *I'm sure people have always missed their mothers.*

Treak had taken off his last-of-summer hat. His first-of-winter hat, gorgeous with arctic fox fur, blew white and crisp in the ice-chilled wind from the north. Treak's change of hat was a sure sign of snow.

The retreat to the caves of Mended Vision that winter wasn't planned. The snows were unusually heavy when they came, that cutting winter of 7650 BC, the year my mother died of a gangrenous leg. I liked to think of her joining my father around a feast made up of all their favourite things. That was how I liked to think of them together, but sometimes it all got mixed up – especially when I was drifting off to sleep. Then my father would take the swan's wing from behind his ochre-stained head and eat it, and my mother would have no legs at all – or two that weren't hers – and all the food they were eating was rotten, you could see if you looked really closely. Then the Beast would shake me. *Shut up. You're having a nightmare.*

I had quite a few nightmares, those first few days in Mended Vision. Maybe it was the echoing galleries deep in the back of the cave, maybe it was some of the stuff I'd been through. Argos treated me like eggshell. He didn't ask any questions. He didn't make any rules. I tried to explain about the amber bear; the way I'd felt; the way I'd wanted to tell him. Then I talked about Mum. On and on about Mum. Argos listened and nodded, big enough to take it all, not judging, not probing, just listening. The silences between me and Argos spoke more than a day-long wrangle with anyone else. They were thick, understanding silences. Maybe he guessed how much they meant. It took my dad's death to make me never want to care about anything ever again, it took my mother's to bring me home. I don't know what I'd've done if Argos had given me a hard time. I might've

Climbed the Sky and kept on going, the way I felt after Mum died.

The god Naal is a vengeful god, a god of fire and ice. Arf's warning went round and round in my head at a time when fire meant life or death. That winter of 7650 really caught us on the hop. Everything was wet. Everything was cold. Pre-Boreal winters were usually kind. No one had stored or seasoned birchwood for burning. No one had even thought about it. Everyone managed the best way they could, miserably scrounging odds and ends, mainly freezing slowly. I don't know if you've ever tried lighting a fire with freeze-dried sodden birchwood? I don't recommend it. It's not the most rewarding thing you can do. Argos and I found an old cave-bear's nest in the labyrinths of Mended Vision. We were lucky. The mound of dry sticks and bracken kept us going a long while.

No one knew if the Olds were OK. No one even asked. No one talked much about anything except windfall carrion and tinder. Now and again, out collecting wood, I heard a whisper or two, mainly about the Pits. The never-ending aggro brought on by the Leaderene's treachery after the Contest raged on a long while. The sandpits had changed hands more than once or twice. Gargas lost most of his hair in an incident involving a flaming boar's head. I'm hazy about the details, but I think most of it was down to Gargas himself. Sometimes the Axes were in possession, sometimes Viger's Horde. I lost interest after a while. Helping to feed five in sub-zero temperatures tends to take up most of your time, you know? Last I heard, the Pits had dug in for the winter. They were desperate for food. Almost everyone was.

The cutting winter winds had changed everything, clothing Climbing Sky in sparkling white. Trees loaded with snow would dump on anyone who brushed them. Worse still, sensing a hard winter, any remaining deer had taken off south with the geese. Even the Bedeviller had come in from the cold, occupying a little-visited cave in a part of Mended Vision filled with bones. Mainly mammoth bones. Treak ground medicines and sang to himself, and nothing worried him greatly, not even Eels. She joined him sometimes, her plans to rob and crush the Bedeviller strangely frozen along with everything else. The snows that year were a last blast from the Ice Age, changing hopes and dreams with the landscape, setting the lake like an eye in a socket, unblinking, unmoving, shot with ice-locked canoes.

Food and fire were Argos' continuing mission. First he smashed the ice like the others and spear-fished sluggish trout. When the ice got too thick to smash he joined the hunting party. The hunting party specialized in digging out bear cubs hibernating under the snow. Soon they were all dug out. The odd arctic hare came our way, but divided between the hunting party, there wasn't enough left to flavour a pot of melted snow. The morning Argos finally left, over a breakfast of three-day-old mussel chowder, I told Bee he wouldn't be away long.

"Anyway," I comforted, "he'll be back before you know it. Probably bring us a side of elk, maybe even reindeer. Like reindeer, dontcha?"

Four-year-old Bee nodded seriously. "Argos be back. An' I want."

"Want what?"

"Want Ma."

"You *know* about that. I *told* you Mam Climbed the Sky. So don't…"

Broddha shot me a warning look. Being all together in a hungry heap wasn't going to be easy.

"So don't worry," I finished lamely. "'Cos we're all here to look after you."

"When *will* Argos be back?" asked the Beast.

"How do I know? Soon."

The truth was, I didn't know when it would be. The hunting party had been preparing for a major hunt for a while. That morning, the morning they finally left, I watched them stoking the dogs for the trip with strips of inedible ox-hide. It always amazed me what dogs would eat. They'd been eating each other, lately. Even the elk had been reduced to sucking lichen off the rocks before they'd wandered south. I tried lichen myself, in a bad moment. It was a bit like eating soil-flavoured tripe. I didn't try it again.

Argos had braced me with a man-to-wimp talk that morning before he left. It's up to you, Broddy. Keep 'em safe. Keep 'em warm. Be back before you know it. I nodded, choked, used to dealing in silences. Argos squared my shoulders with his great big hands and understood. He handed me the amber bear. I knew what it meant. The silence between us that morning had been one that no one dared break. The girls had waved him off with solemn hugs and kisses. Even the Beast had been subdued.

I watched the hunt wink away over the snow-loaded Olds' ridge, to a valley crowded (they hoped) with wintering deer and ibex. Ma Fingers watched them, too. I watched her, watching. The Fingers' cave was too close to ours by a mile. Occupying her ancestors' winter retreat like she was a throwback herself, Ma Fingers let everyone know she, if everyone *else* froze, would survive the winter the way her forebears had.

I nodded to her. "'Lo."

Ma Fingers ignored me, scouting after the hunting party with mean little frost-ringed eyes. Just how dangerous was she? Would she slip over to Eels? With the Pits near-starving they wouldn't need too much encouragement to rob what little, or nothing, we had. Better, by far, Ma Fingers stayed at home. I watched Ma Fingers a while. Then I got up and fetched something.

Taking the remains of the mussel chowder over, I gave Ma Fingers the best good morning I could, with Argos lengthening the distance between us by the minute.

"Got some over. Too good to waste." I didn't

bother with the niceties. You don't, with snow-chapped lips.

Ma Fingers eyed me over the bowl, draining it completely before she answered. "Broddy Brodson. Trying times for us all."

She looked pretty rough. Even the bracket-fungus hairstyle had wilted. I felt the tiniest twinge of guilt as she handed me back the bowl.

"Stub and Falco gone with the hunt?"

Ma Fingers rubbed her (only) front tooth with her finger. "They're good boys. They'll bring us a head of aurochs."

I hoped not, wondering, uneasily, where Ur was wintering this year.

"Lookee, Broddy." Ma Fingers beckoned me closer. "Lookee what I got here." Lifting the reed-mat she was squatting on, she reached down into a hole in the cave-floor, feeling for something hidden. The onyx hammer she pincered out was heavy, ornate – and familiar.

"The Burial Committee hammer?" I hadn't seen it in a long while.

"They been looking everywhere for this one." Ma Fingers rocked with glee. "I pinched it in the move."

"So. You can't eat hammers."

"No, but you c'n hit folk with 'em – eh, Broddy?" Ma Fingers winked grotesquely, hooking me closer with her claw. "What say, Broddy, eh? Eh?"

Sad, mad Ma Fingers. She finally went over the

edge; that winter so many people had to come down on one side or the other. Much later, breaking the ice on a fishing hole where there were no fish, I got to thinking. Everything was up in the air, including – especially – my future. With our parents dead, what future was there for me and the girls around the lake? The same future as anywhere else, I supposed. Harsh winters and sudden death could come anywhere, anytime – but something like a half-remembered song tugged in the back of my mind. *When Mam goes over the ridge, me an' Bee's going over the mountain if we want to. When Mam goes over the ridge…*

I looked up. The summit of Climbing Sky lowered over its snow-weighted crags and passes. I searched its unfriendly face, the way I had before. Somewhere under the ice shelf, Viger said. Somewhere under the grim-looking ice shelf under the summit there lay a way over, Horl Stendevenger told him. Whoever Horl Stendevenger was.

An' over there it's honey every day. An' me an' Bee's goin' if we want to. Honeyland-over-the-mountain. Who was it said? The Beast.

12

In the Batcave – Gang of One – The Secret of Mended Vision

Grub Fingers approached across the ice. I watched him with disgust, not least because of his too-disgusting mother. There was no easy way to avoid him. Sitting beside the single useable fishing hole on the lake, there wasn't a whole lot to hide behind. His twisted-hazel vole-traps swinging on his back, Grub Fingers walked right up and said what he had to say:

"A message from Viger. Watch your back. The Pits are about to attack. Again. They could hit you any time."

I opened my mouth, then closed it. "You tell them the men's gone away?"

"Would I?" Grub Fingers spread his hands innocently. His missing fingers made the gesture about as convincing as his tone. "Broddy. You know me."

That was all of the trouble. I knew Grub only too well. I might've known he'd stir it, even if Ma stayed home. The Fingers were monsters of self-interest, down to their least most-cut-offable bones. It looked as though the Axes had no choice, after all. Raid or be raided, what to do? The Leaderene would know. The Leaderene, with her snapping black eyes and decisive, military mind. I hadn't seen her in a long while. I wasn't even exactly sure where she was. Somewhere in the east-frowning face of Mended Vision, where most of the bats hung out.

My beaver-wrapped feet polished the ice as I walked. The ice on the lake that year was all of two metres thick in some places. Other places, it wasn't so thick. Coarse and uneven as one of Arf's bowls of porridge, some parts of the ice creaked and bled water through freaky-looking cracks that tended to whiplash together. Extreme caution was needed to walk a straight line, especially when you noticed all the things that hadn't. The ice was like a frozen natural history museum. Pressured into gruesome shapes, the bodies of all the creatures that had fallen in and frozen looked sadly up through murky layers of lakewater. Frozen fishes boggled, weed fanned and twisted. All along the margins the reed-beds had stiffened like spears, the ice around them spongy underfoot where frosted rafts of watercress, the texture of Needcliff's moustache, made an interesting border.

As I walked, I thought. Viger had sent me a message. A message to save myself. Viger thought I'd save me and mine when the Pits raided Mended

Vision, leaving everyone else (just their bad luck) to cop it. There was a time when I might've. Not any more. I wasn't perfect any more, the way I'd been in the Pits – perfectly unfeeling to everything, and everyone, around me. Since Mum's death brought me home, since Argos' acceptance let me live with it, I was further away from perfect than I'd ever be. I wasn't about to nick off and leave everyone else to get grazed over, whatever Viger, reading me wrong, had thought. It wasn't until much later I realized Grub Fingers had read me right.

Thinking all of this and more, I climbed to Mended Vision. A place of knocks and cracks and whispers, sudden laughter and the chink of flint on flint, Mended Vision at that time was fuller with spirits, alive and dead, than it had ever been before. Passing the flint-filled cavern where the clan Gargas had its noisy core-axe operation, jumping the stream which pounded through tunnels and sumps in the blackness under the mountain where nothing moved or breathed, I entered a gallery known as the batcave, on account of the bats.

The Leaderene sat huddled in the (only bright) corner with Vert. Vert turned as I entered the gallery. I looked up. The darkness above glistened with bats' eyes. The rustle and fidget of two, maybe three thousand, bats made me feel more than a little claustrophobic. Hanging room only, I thought. The roof overhead was chockers. In case you hadn't looked up, the dung underneath was a giveaway. An age-old mound of bat-droppings and mummified bat-infants who'd failed the upside-down test was the main decorative feature on offer. The other was the single shaft of daylight under the twisted limestone funnel – where the bats flickered in and out – giving onto the furthermost corner of the cave. The Leaderene hogged all the light. It looked as though she needed it. It didn't take a genius to see there was something wrong with her eyes.

"What's up with her eyes?"

Vert looked severe. "She's injured, OK?"

"I didn't know. I'm sorry."

Vert sneered. "What *do* you know?"

"I know you think I'm slugslime."

"You came here to tell me that?"

"Plus."

"Plus what?"

"Plus I know the Pits are about to attack."

"Who says?" The Leaderene cocked her head.

"Grub Fingers. He told me to watch my back."

"He tell anyone else?"

"He told *me*. Now I'm telling you. Could happen any time."

"No." The Leaderene jumped up, her eyes working blindly under sealed-up eyelids. The circle of light on her face showed me how bad the damage was. Remembering those sharp black eyes, I didn't really want to see. "We've still got a chance with surprise on our side," she said. "There must be a way to get back at them first. Let me think."

"How did she get like this?" I asked Vert softly. "Tell me the way it was."

Vert shrugged. "We make a few raids on the Pits' camp. She plans them all, except one time – one time she comes up behind Cud? That Cud, he throws burning lime in her face. Shoulda seen her eyes the day after."

I swallowed. "Does she see?"

Vert shook his head. "Not much. They get gummed up."

I watched the Leaderene thinking. "What d'you think she'll do?"

"About the Pits?"

"We can't go on like this. Scared they'll attack all the time."

The Leaderene cleared her throat to indicate she'd reached a decision. "They've got the approaches covered. We'll have to walk over the lake."

"Walk over the lake?" Vert boggled. "Excuse me? Over the ice?"

"If you know any other way to walk over the lake, let me know."

It was good to hear that flat tone again. Good to see the Leaderene smiling that wry smile, the smile that said she was right, and it was only a matter of time before you took her point.

Vert took it, slowly. "They've posted lookouts both sides of the lake ... canoes are iced in until spring ... looks like we don't have a choice."

I said, "But they'll see us coming. We'll fall through the ice."

"Not under cover of night. If we fall through the ice, we fall."

"We won't do that," said Arf. "I c'n pick a way across."

Peeling himself off a rock grey with bat-droppings, Arf joined us in the circle of light pooling in the corner under the bat-funnel. I'd had no idea he was there. He looked different, somehow. Less manic. There was a kind of stillness about him I hadn't noticed before. I hadn't seen Arf in a long while. Not since the Ordeal by Strength and Endurance, that fish-net-tightening day the late summer shadows had lengthened over the crossroads. Arf had changed since then.

"If you come at 'em another way as well, I c'n pick a way across the ice," repeated Arf.

"I like it." The Leaderene nodded slowly. "Now we're getting somewhere."

"I'll lead a party around the back of the dunes," I told her. The "seeing as you can't" hung unspoken. "We can hit the coast way north of the sandpits, work our way down around the beach-head, come up over 'em the back way, no worries."

"Just like that," said Vert dryly.

The Leaderene considered. Her eyes worked under their lids, remembering something. "Broddy Brodson. Take the Axes' oath again."

"I take no oaths. I stand alone." It sounded pretty dramatic, but I meant it.

"Me too." Arf grinned. "That's what I do, kind of."

"We noticed," Vert said. "Let us know when you're thinking of dobbing us in to the Pits again, will you? So we can feed you a line?"

"I'm not doing that any more," said Arf sadly. "Naal strike me dead if I do."

"I wouldn't tempt fate," said Vert.

"How about you?" the Leaderene asked softly. "Can we trust you, Broddy Brodson?"

"Hey," I told her, "I got three little sisters, next cave along to the Fingers'. Like, I'm going to put them in danger, or something? I don't want any trouble. I want the trouble to stop."

The Leaderene nodded, satisfied. Then she spoke quickly, quietly, to no one in particular, thinking aloud, letting us share the workings of a keen and practical mind.

"We take a hostage, maybe Wildgoose himself, we force a truce. A classic pincer movement, closing on the dunes, and we might have Wildgoose *and* the camp ... fresh shellfish all winter, plus a token occupation force gives us first option on the sandpits next spring. Raid or be raided, that's how it stands..."

I watched the others, watching the Leaderene. It felt good to be back in the Axes again, except that I wasn't. It felt good, at least, to be a part of something not based on thieving. If I stood alone, I stood for *something*. The first and only Gang of One.

That night in the cave, a thought occurred. The fire

flickered low, my sleeping sisters huddled together under Argos' elkhide greatcoat, their breath steaming over them and freezing onto its edges like hoarfrost. Practically lying on top of the fire for warmth, I got to thinking. As cold as it was for us, how was it over the ridge?

The Olds had been on my mind, on and off, for a long time. The truth was, I wasn't too proud of myself. My part in the ram-raid on the Olds' ridge had been less than central, but all the same it bothered me in a way that I'd forgotten something you'd done some time ago could. I suppose you'd call it an attack of conscience. As Grub would say, it was giving me stick. It had nothing to do with eating mussels, and no amount of sleeping near the stream would wash it away.

I re-ran the raid in slow motion. After a while the scene unfolded itself again and again, whether I wanted it to or not: the pine logs, smashing down the slope, wiping the Olds' bivouac off the ridge like it'd never existed; the general panic as they scattered; the single old bloater trying to untie his dog from a post before taking off, his fumbling old fingers bodging the job, his fearful eyes popping so we thought he'd drop dead and save us the trouble; the old girl running with a basket of quail chicks, a pet polecat bobbing across her shoulders; the chapped old war-hero making his stand with a digging stick, roaring: *I'll tan their hides! Hooligans! Vandals! I'll give 'em a taste of what they're missing!*

We hadn't really taken much; there hadn't been that much to take. It was a laugh, right? It'd been funny for us while it lasted, but had it been kind? The Olds came crowding in on me, whichever way I turned – the fearful old man with his dog, the quail-chick woman, the war-hero. They ringed around to judge me. They wouldn't leave me alone.

Suddenly I got up and went out into the crisp, sub-zero night air. A lone wolf's howl curled around the valley under the moonlight, the kind of lonely, searching call the last wolf on earth would give. It seemed to sum it all up. If I stand alone, I stand for *something*. Checking the cave-mouth once, I started out for the Olds' ridge.

Hayta was taking a pee in the snow outside the family cave when I buzzed him. "Idiot," he said sleepily. "What d'you want to do that for?"

"Because."

"You made me get my feet wet. What's – what are you doing?"

I shrugged. "I was wondering about the Olds. I was wondering about going over the ridge to see how they are."

"Going over the Olds' Ridge? In the middle of the night?"

"People don't freeze to death when it's convenient. They do it all the time."

"I suppose." Hayta searched my eyes.

"Come with me?"

"What for?"

"I can use you."

Hayta nodded. "OK."

Snatching an ibex cover-all from the cave-mouth, Hayta came after me. We worked our way around the path, normally OK, but this weather slippy as bear-grease. We were actually working our way around the base of Climbing Sky. It was a bit like edging around a giant iced cake, with nothing much to stop you from skittering way down onto the plate, or frozen lake, below. We finally left Mended Vision behind us. The cave-mouths looked like a row of bad teeth in the white lower slopes of the mountain. I looked up. The mountain was practically on top of us. Way above us the first snow-field reached up in the night sky. Beyond it towered an ice-cliff. It looked like one ice-cliff too far.

After a longish traverse we made a left turn. The path dropped away to circle the north-west side of the lake before climbing up to the Olds' ridge. I liked the sound of Hayta's friendly footfall behind me, out under the hard-faced stars. Standing alone was good, but standing together was better. The lone wolf's call set the ridge ringing as we crossed its flanks, our hide-bound feet compacting the snow with a squeak. I hoped we were clear of sabre-tooths. They were active, moonlit nights. Not for the first time, I wished I'd brought my spear.

It took longer than we thought it would to climb the Olds' ridge. Covered as it was with black ice from top to bottom, I wondered how the Olds came up and down. Maybe they didn't in this weather. Hayta certainly did. He went up, then down, two or three times. By the time I'd handed him up to a foothold the fourth time, I was almost wishing him home in bed.

"Come on, clumsy-klutz."

"I *would*, if you'd move on up."

We crossed the snow-field that climbed on up to the spine of the ridge side by side, not talking at all, just thinking. We'd been through a lot of stuff together, Hayta and I. There were things between Hayta and I that neither one of us needed to talk about to know they were real. More real than ever, tonight. Up there on the Olds' ridge, with the frozen valley stretching below us and no sound but the steady crunch of both our feet in the snow, it seemed like we were the best and only mates in the world. I looked at Hayta. Maybe he felt it, too.

Hayta looked up. Then he said, "I can't believe we're doing this. It's not so long ago I thought you were the pits of the *world*."

"I was. But I've changed now. Really."

"Really?"

I held out my hand. "Believe it."

My switch to the Pits had hit Hayta hard. We slapped hands. Hayta grinned. He wanted to believe it.

After a while I said, "If I said I was going some-where, would you come?"

Hayta stopped. "Going where?"

144

"Somewhere. Over the mountain. There's a way."

Hayta stared. "Over the mountain? Why?"

"Why not?"

"I mean, why would you go?"

"Mum and Dad're gone. What's to stay for?"

"Your sisters. Argos. Me."

We walked on a while in silence. Then I said, "I wouldn't go alone. Me and the girls, we'd go together. Argos, he's got his own kids. In any case, we'd visit. It's not like we'd go for ever."

"You got it all planned out, then." Hayta came near to being bitter.

I stopped. "It isn't a plan. It's just that there's got to be something better. Another place to live, a different way of doing things, you know?"

Hayta nodded. "I know," he said at last.

"So would you?"

"Go over the mountain?" Hayta shook his head. "How would I know what was on the other side?"

"That's the whole point. You wouldn't."

"I haven't got it, Broddy. You know I'm not like you."

"Sometimes I don't think anyone else *is*."

"You said it." Hayta pushed me. "You're mad, you are."

I pushed him back. "I'll miss you."

"No, you won't."

"I will."

"Don't talk about it any more, all right?"

145

"If you want."

"I want."

"OK."

"OK."

"Right."

We finally reached the spine of the ridge. Sloping away on its far side, the scene of the ram-raid on the Olds opened in front of me. I had to remind myself where I was. The jumble of snow-covered lumps didn't look much like Oldstown. Then I remembered. We hadn't left much of it standing. This was the very slope we'd crashed the logs down. All that was left of the dismal outpost the Olds called – *had* called – home was a mess of crooked posts and punctured benders thickly covered with snow. Nothing moved on that ridge except a few fluttering goatskins. No one lived there any more. No one called it home.

"Looks like they cleared out." Hayta pulled me after him. "Might as well take a look now we're here."

I supposed we might as well. Hayta went on ahead, knocking shelves of powder-snow off stove-in hovels, kicking tents, shouting in every other bender. I followed slowly, glad no one was freezing to death in the sad remains of Oldstown. Or so I thought.

"Wow. Hey. Get this." Hayta turned and shouted.

Get this. I caught him up crossly, wondering how come Hayta was so sure-footed all of a sudden, where the knocked-up footings of huts and tents destroyed in the raid made me feel less than wonderful.

Hayta pointed. "Take a look in there."

"Where?"

"In there. No kidding. Look in."

I ducked partly inside what looked like a snow-covered heap of mammoth bones, but was, in fact, a hut. The single grizzled old woman inside it looked pretty mean to me. Her mouth worked busily, gathering spit. I just pulled out before she gobbed me one.

"Arf's mother – isn't it?" asked Hayta.

"She won't last long in there," I said. "Better get her out."

Here was the token Old I needed to make me feel better about all the rest. It would be a heart-warming job to rehouse her. Hauling Arf's tooth-less mother out of her hut, I made up my mind to do right by her even though she stank, mainly of bear-fat, the kind of bear-fat that hadn't seen a bear in a long while. Old Mother Haagerbarta was rancid *and* stroppy, if you really want to know. You'd have thought she didn't *want* to be rescued. Lucky for us she was light.

"Murthur!" she squawked, as we dragged her out. "Murthur, I thay! Murthur!"

"What's she say?" I asked Hayta.

"Search me," said Hayta. "Does she want her mother?"

"Her *mother*?" I boggled. "I should think her mother's snuffed it, wouldn't you?"

"More than," agreed Hayta. "Let's get 'er down an' away."

Going down the black-ice path from the snow-field, we rolled her in Hayta's ibex-quilt and slugged her to and fro between us over the ice, going down a foothold or three in turn, keeping a tight grip on the tied-up ends, watching for straying arms or legs or any signs of escape. Knew she was being rescued, didn't she? Arf's toothless mother didn't struggle much.

She didn't look too grateful when we unwrapped her at the bottom. Hayta explained we were sorry about that, but it was for her own good. After she smacked him I rolled her up again quickly, so all she could do was shout. She shouted quite a lot. Then she settled down. What lucky old-timer wouldn't?

Dragging Mother Haagerbarta between us, we crossed the flank of the ridge. We let her travel the last bit down to the lake under her own steam. Might as well let 'er rip, said Hayta, pointing out there wasn't a lot of sense in dragging her when she could roll. Hayta bet she'd spiral off left in the pines, but I bet she'd cut a straight line. We watched her roll all the way down to the lake. She built up quite a bit of speed. She was really cooking when she finally stopped at the bottom. After we dragged her around the edge of the lake we started the climb to Mended Vision. It felt like Arf's toothless mother got heavier, the further we hauled her. It just about killed us, getting her up.

She was easier to drag now she'd gone quiet. Probably she'd got used to it.

I felt a lot better about myself now I'd done something. I pictured Arf's face when he saw his mother. I thought about the last time I'd seen him, in the Batcave. I thought about the battle plans; the bats' eyes; the sightless Leaderene.

Then I said: "Shame about the Leaderene's eyes."

"They're only gummed up," said Hayta.

"I dunno. Burning lime. Looks a lot worse than that."

Hayta nodded. "I know it looks bad. Maybe that'll show her."

"Show her what?"

"Fighting never solved anything."

"Oh. And you never did it?"

"I haven't done it in a long while. I'm not in the Axes now."

"No?"

"I dropped it. Can't see the point."

"The point is, the Axes are all we've got. The Pits're coming over, didn't you know?"

"A raid?" Hayta stopped. "No one tells me anything."

"We're all on battle standby. Win or lose, it's the end this time."

Hayta thought. "When's the battle?"

"Three days' time. Surprise attack."

The glow of togetherness was wearing off a little. By the time we reached the part of Mended

Vision which held Arf's toothless mother's favourite son, I was tired and cross and muddled. *Fighting never solved anything.* I was beginning to think arguing never solved anything, least of all with Hayta. Arguing with Hayta was like arguing with myself.

Arf's toothless mother stirred when we set her down in the cave-mouth. Hayta unwrapped her warily. She looked around, remembering.

"Mended Vithion. Good for eyeth."

"What's she say?" I wondered.

"Mended Vision. Good for eyes. She talks weird because of her teeth."

I suspected it was more because she had *no* teeth. "You don't have to stay," I told Hayta. "I'm leaving her here and getting Arf."

Hayta nodded. He watched Mother Haagerbarta's face. He squatted beside her. She smacked him smartly. "Robberth. Raiderth. Thugth."

Hayta stood up quickly. "Moody, in't she?" Then he said, "Reckon she was saying 'murder' before?"

"When?"

"When we pulled her out of her hut. I reckon she was shouting 'murder' not 'mother'."

"Why would she want to shout murder when we were rescuing her?"

"Ask *her*. Miserable old ratbag. She's lucky I saw her. Might have frozen to death."

Thoroughly rescued, and not quite as hostile, Old Mother Haagerbarta sat straight abruptly. She beckoned Hayta closer.

Hayta nudged me. "She wants you."

"She doesn't. She wants *you*."

"I'm not bending over. She always hits me."

Old Mother Haagerbarta beckoned and nodded. It might be something important, I thought. Better find out what she wants.

I nudged Hayta back. "She wants to tell you something, can't you see?"

Hayta considered. "It better be good."

Bending warily, holding his nose, Hayta put his ear to Old Mother Haagerbarta's mouth. He listened carefully to what she had to say. Then he tried to tell me.

"The one with burning lime in her eyeth, to bathe in Mended Vithion," he relayed. " 'Least she never hit me."

"The one with burning lime in her eyes, to bathe in Mended Vision," I translated, the meaning dawning slowly. I searched Mother Haagerbarta's face. "You mean what we were saying about the Leaderene? You mean the water in the caves...?"

Hayta bent again. Then he straightened. "*Under the mountain, where the healing waters flow...* Know what else she says? She says, You kids these days know nothing. Us old-timers knew the mountain when you kids was widdling in the willows. *Why d'you think it's called Mended Vision?*"

13

A Stone Age Rave – The Omen

I took all three girls to the eve-of-battle party. When Bee fell asleep in the dip we went home. On the way back to the cave I liberated the Burial Committee hammer from under Ma Fingers' mat, and didn't feel bad about doing it at all. A hammer like that deserved to do something a little more heroic than calling the Burial Committee to order. Ma Fingers wasn't at home. She'd been ill in the bushes ever since the morning the hunt left. Sometimes she'd emerge, a bit shaken. She'd straighten her back and pass the time of day. Then she'd change colour and rush off mid-sentence. Ma Fingers blamed old mussel chowder. Old mussel chowder could take you that way, said Ma Fingers. Treak's bedevilment potions were pretty subtle. It ended up she *lived* in the bushes. The wolf-headed god had struck her down for her wickedness at last, ran the rumour. Hadn't Ma Fingers stood by and watched her own aged mother sold for a packhorse by her, Ma Fingers', *own son*? Naal's Revenge was swift and sure. I wasn't sorry. Hadn't she tried to cut my finger off?

No one missed Ma Fingers much except Grub, who popped in now and again with warnings of imminent attack and battle preparations in the sandpits. We'd been through a few battle preparations of our own. The Leaderene outlined basic strategy at the party to anyone who would listen. There were five points to basic battle strategy. Most people who didn't dance at parties had decided maybe they would listen, by point three. Me, I listened until she ran down, watching those flashing black eyes emphasize each point. *1. Concentration. 2. Surprise. 3. Co-operation. 4. Mobility. 5. Luck.* These were the five main principles. The first four were down to good leadership, the fifth to all the gods. *Concentration*, on all the enemy's weak points; *Surprise*, in a feinted attack to disguise a real one; *Co-operation*, as all parts of the "army" work as one; *Mobility*, in moving faster than the enemy; *Luck*, as in taking advantage of opportunities. If two sides were fairly equal in strength, explained the Leaderene, that side would nearly always win which kept more closely to the five principles. Neglect them and die, snapped her lively black eyes.

Did I say lively black eyes? Old Mother Haagerbarta had bathed them herself, in a deep and secret mineral pool in the heart of Mended Vision. OK, she threw in a few incantations as well, maybe some birch antiseptic – but it was mainly the water that did it. In only two days the Leaderene's eyes had been opened. In three, they'd widened and focused. Clear-sighted before, she saw more clearly than anyone the way things were between Arf and his mother.

Arf and his mother had been less than delighted with each other. Some kind of row blew up involving a lot of shouting about Arf's hairstyle, never the best. Old Mother Haagerbarta had sniffily taken up residence in the batcave with the Leaderene as a result. The Leaderene sniped at Arf at every opportunity, as a relief from Mother Haagerbarta's gummy conversation. The three of them went round and round in a dance of tangled feelings, each annoying the other, Arf more than most. By day three it got a bit spiteful. The Leaderene threw the thing she valued most – a ritual baton carved with horses' heads – into the sinister-looking cave-pool which had saved her sight, as a gift to all the secret, wide-eyed gods of Mended Vision. Arf fished it out again, later. No reason. I saw him with it after. We exchanged a look. I knew how he felt, I really did.

Battle plans were revised. Now that she could see, the Leaderene would lead the assault around the back of the dunes. Me? I was to close the pincers with the expedition over the ice-bound lake with Arf "second sight" Haagerbarta for a guide. I only hoped he'd pick a way over the ice better'n he picked out a rhythm. I told him so at the eve-of-battle party, through the deaf-making clump of the drums.

"Arf," I bellowed, "*I* could drum better than that."

"Sorry?" Arf looked up, hitting an off-beat every three to four seconds, completely out of sync with everyone else, like he was drumming to some private rhythm in his head. "What's that you said, Broddy?"

"You're all over the place. Even *I* could keep time better."

"Here." Arf jumped up. He handed me his antler drum-hammer, making me keep it when I tried to hand it back. "No. Broddy. I want you to."

I sat down and took Arf's place in the band. Half a dozen drums made a pulse like a heartbeat under the torches lining the cave walls. You could call it the original jam session. A real Pre-Boreal thrash. Most of the instruments were handed-down mammoth-bone rattlers, drums or xylophones of one kind or another, polished with age and well-treasured, plus one or two reindeer toe-bone whistles to lead the breaks. I don't guess you've been to a Stone Age rave. It's kind of like any you go to, except there's no charge for water and no one busts you on the way there. Gargas chanted loudly over the backbeat, eyes closed, arms out like he was swimming through fish-glue. Gargas fancied himself as a vocalist. He had on blue-black oxhide, plus he'd painted his scalp blue to match. Pretty soon he'd be head-banging. Gargas had no shame.

Gargas posed; the drummers drummed; the torches crackled blue with salt, green with copper-ore. Everyone else forgot themselves in the dance. The heart of the drumbeat thickened, solo drums cresting and falling, spirit-shakers swishing in the breaks. Those Stone Age rhythms washed over me. I don't know how long I drummed for. I don't know how long the ravers raved, how far the night wore on. Around about the time the advance party left for the coast I noticed my sister Bee asleep in the lichen dip. I princess-carried her up and collared the others. Then I found Arf in the cloakcave amongst the cloaks.

I gave him the antler drum-hammer. "That's about it for tonight."

Arf grinned sleepily. "Get some kip if you can."

"Hope you know what you're up for, Arf. Think you know the ice?"

"Not the ice, Broddy. Myself."

I looked at Arf sharply. "What did you say?"

Too wise to say it again, Arf sank back in the wolf-pelts no one could be bothered to claim. *Not the ice, Broddy. Myself.* Had he really said it? It sounded way too wise for Arf. But he'd changed a lot, I remembered. I wasn't giving him credit. There was more to Arf than I thought.

"The platform. See you there." Arf smiled. His eyes were closed. In sleep, he'd still be smiling.

"See you there," I told him.

Now the party was over. I sat up late, alone. Just me and my shadow. And the Burial Committee hammer. It was a nice hammer, the Burial Committee hammer. Its birch-wood shaft had been hardened in the fire so it would never shrink from holding up the figured onyx head. The figured onyx head showed an aurochs in light relief. Quite skilful, as it goes. After I put Bee down I showed it to the Beast before she went to bed, explaining how I'd use it in battle next day. Mainly for stunning, I told her. Capturing Viger was high on the agenda. Any hostages would help to keep the peace, especially Cud. I was looking forward to meeting Cud again. So was the Leaderene.

Broddha was in charge until I got back. She took her role pretty seriously. "You should go to bed now, else you'll be tired in the morning," she told the Beast self-righteously.

" 'Be tired if I want to, an' I *want* to." The Beast scowled. "Jus' 'cos *you* be good, doesn't mean *I'm* bein' good as well."

"I think it does." I tapped the Beast on her forehead. "How can I be off sorting things out if I know you're home playing everyone up?"

"Doesn't matter anyway what I do 'cos you're not coming back." The Beast zipped up her mouth.

"Say *what*?"

"You're goin' in battle, give Viger a hammerin', you are."

"What makes you think I won't come back?"

"Dad went away and *he* never. Mam never came back. Now you're goin' away, an' I do whatever I want. Because."

"Because you're Miss Ninny of Stupidland?"

The Beast grinned. "Am not."

"Are. That's where you live. Stupidland."

"Where *you* live, silly boys come and put rubbish on your head."

"Rubbish on *your* head." I pushed her. "And when I come back, I'm going to put rubbish down your back."

"Are not."

"Am. All down your back. You wait."

I tickled her into bed. At last she fell asleep. I sat up polishing the Burial Committee hammer, thinking over the things she'd said until it was time to go. Dad went away and never came back. Mam went away and never came back. Now *I* was going away, somewhere she wasn't too sure of. I couldn't blame the Beast for thinking I'd disappear for ever. She was only six years old, and acting like it tonight. *Doesn't matter anyway what I do 'cos you're not coming back.* Phew. It wasn't the best eve-of-battle omen I could've imagined.

Time to go. Concentration. Surprise. Co-operation. Mobility. Luck.

Lodging the Burial Committee hammer in my belt along with my daggers, I took a last long look at the girls. All asleep. All warm, all safe, all together. All my sisters, Naal keep 'em. Then I walked out through the last-of-night stillness to the rendezvous at the platform.

14

Over the Lake – Fire and Ice – The Kill

"Shee – oot, it's softer'n a dawg's belly!" Treak broke the ice first. Literally. "Help me, boys, I'm sinking!"

Crossing the lake on the ice, scrabbling for a foothold, falling flat and sinking, the Bedeviller had hit a weak spot. Snaking him a catgut line, we caught him before his hat went under, hauling him out on the ice like a big wet fish. He rolled around cursing his luck, the lake, the ice, his boots, the night and most of creation. He made the most of it, he really did, considering we risked our lives. He was way out of line, in any case. No one told him to wander off, like he knew a better way over the ice. It was just about as bad as it could be since Treak carried, *did* carry, most of the spears – now lancing down to an early grave on the lake-bed, where Simps would rejoice in them nine thousand years later.

"Well done," I told him. "Brilliant. Now we lost the spears."

"Dang an' blast them sealskin boots to the bottom o' the sea, they got me slidin' like a one-fin fish on a line, I never got no good luck yet out o' seal boots, curse 'em for foot-stranglers – "

"*Must* you make so much noise?" Vert looked at Treak severely. "It's your own fault. You should've stuck behind Arf."

"If *you* had half a gut fulla ice-water, like to freeze to death, I betcha *you'd* whine a little."

"Don't say that." Arf paled through his warpaint. "I don't want to think about freezing to death. I've been thinking a lot about it lately."

Treak had hit a nerve. I looked at Arf. He looked as though a ghost, or at least the shadow of a ghost, had just walked over his grave.

"Get up and shut up," I told Treak crossly. "You're making everyone nervous."

"Looks like there's a sea-mist coming in." Gargas' brother squinted ahead. "Let's hope they haven't heard us."

"What do we do when we get there?" asked Dug. "I mean, now we lost most of the spears?"

"I've still got mine. What'll you do?" Vert raised both eyebrows. "Give 'em a nasty smack?"

"We'll improvise," I told him. "Lead on Arf, you're doing good."

Arf led on. He *was* doing good. Better, by a mile, than I could, especially through last-of-night. The only-just-visible ice seemed cloudy instead of transparent, green instead of grey. Every day it looked different. Every day the cracks in it ran together. Arf moved in a mysterious way, picking a path across the ice by radar, religion or dead reckoning. No one asked him how he did it. No one questioned the route. Even the Bedeviller followed on meekly, having wandered off line and suffered for it once. Arf "second sight" Haagerbarta had his ways and means. So long as they worked, no one was about to upset his seer's bowl of mysteries. There were more things in heaven and earth than were dreamt of by us or anyone else, and one of them was Arf.

I pictured the advance party's night journey down the coast, not envying them the long and difficult trek over snow-laden dunes with the sea whipping the beaches, frozen auks and puffins rolling like stones in the breakers to remind them how easily – how very easily – we could *all* go belly side up. The moon would show them the way, but would it show them the Pits, unsuspectingly asleep in their dugouts and warrens? I hoped so. I really did. I'm not one for bloodshed, I'm really not. I was hoping we could all get back for root-tea and rollmop herring that night beside the fire.

With three hours' start on us, I calculated the Leaderene's advance party would be more or less in position on the beaches behind the sandpits by the time we reached the lake-shore in front of them. Those accompanying the Leaderene around the beach-head included: her brother Harrup, her brother Harrup's best mate Stump, Stump's twin sisters (both wrestlers), Gargas, Gargas' meat-partner Woody, Treak's god-daughter with the lucky birthmark on her cheek name of Gundestrup (the god-daughter, not the birthmark), Vert's sister Nesta, and – Simply the Best, Leister the Bowman – next to the Leaderene herself, the best shot in lakeland. Several related bowmen rounded it up to a dozen or more. No Hayta. No Grub Fingers. Hayta had decided going into battle wasn't idealistically sound. Plus he'd left the Axes. Grub Fingers had been carefully excluded.

As the other arm of the pincers that meant to crush the Pits and secure the peace, our party included: Me, Arf, Vert, the Bedeviller, Gargas' brother Rorcus, Rorcus' meat-partner Berk, Berk's cousin Bedgo, Bedgo's mate Turtlejuice, Dug the pimple and a host of minor pimples (male and female) plus Argos' nephew Agerod – quite a useful thrower.

Argos. Seven days since the hunt went away. No meat, no news, no joy. My heart ached, I tell you, at the mention of Argos' name. The least little thing could set me off. A cloak a bit like Argos' cloak, a shadow, a big-hearted laugh. Or the bellow we heard on the ice.

"What's that?" I stopped Arf dead.

The wondering, broken death-call of something fearsome or other rolled around the mountains. I pictured Argos running; Argos the immaculate hunter, deadly as the snake's strike, certain execution in his perfectly-balanced spear. Then I pictured Stub and Falco Fingers stabbing something messily to death. The death-call echoed in the passes and under Climbing Sky, finally drowning in the sea-mist rolling in from the ocean.

"Wow," said Vert. "Maybe the hunt got lucky."

The same thought jumped in all our hungry hearts. *Maybe the hunt got lucky.*

"You still got that three-minute poison?" I asked Vert suddenly, on impulse.

Vert showed me his spear, smug that he'd insisted on carrying it. "Uh-uh." He shook his head. "Don't touch the tip. 'Less you got nothing much on in three minutes' time, or for ever."

Vert's spear-tip spoke of sudden death. Even a scratch would do it. In less time than it took to count thirty-fishes-over-the-weir, Treak's blood-poison would be pumped *by* the heart, *to* the heart – and stop it. The last thing a heart could ever do. Handle With Care, I thought, Vert. It was hard to remember – way back – why the Axes had ever ordered poison in the first place.

I said, "Heavy stuff. Why d'you want to bring it?"

"I've got it, haven't I?" Vert said irritably. "Why not?"

Arf turned. "Can we keep it down now, please? We're getting close. They posted a watch around the camp."

About a quarter-mile from the shoreline, the sea-mist swirled in around us. It was one of those mists you think you'll still be able to see in, just about the time you find you can't. Maybe it was just as well. You know that light between last-of-night and first-of-day? That primrose-white behind grey? It was just beginning to catch us. Pretty soon we'd be as visible as a fly on a bald man's head, with no place to hide but thin ice.

"Fog's closing in," hissed Arf. "Keep together. Pass it on."

"Fog's closing in," hissed Vert. "Keep together. Pass it on."

Treak didn't hear too well. He passed on the message anyway. By the time it reached the end of the line it had pretty much parted company with any sense it started out with.

"Dog's nose is in. Heap toe weather. Basin on. Right." Dug the pimple nodded, mystified. Last in line, he had no one to pass it on to. It wouldn't have been so bad if he'd had an idea what it meant. Perhaps it was some kind of code. The "basin on" part really bothered him.

Clustering close, we went gingerly on through the mist. Soon every direction seemed the same. Everything seemed cold and grey. Everything looked strange. The mist made monsters of everyone, playing tricks with clubs and shields and quivers, attaching them like plates and weird-looking growths to arms and backs and heads, so that no one looked right unless you studied them, and a glance away made them monsters again, only different monsters this time.

"How will we know each other in this fog?" piped Duggie, frightened.

"Shut it," Vert hissed. "We're almost there."

We were closer, by far, than we knew. The lake-bed grounded us unexpectedly, sloping up under our feet through creaking shards of ready-splintered ice.

Arf picked one up. "Look," he said simply. "Spears."

"Good idea." Gargas' brother armed himself with a murderous-looking ice splinter. "Good enough, at least."

They weren't bad. I picked up a shard myself, weighing it against standard spear-weight. It wasn't bad at all.

"OK," I recouped, "when we hit the sandpits we go for it. First to reach Viger Wildgoose sounds their whistle."

The sea-mist closed around us. In moments we lost each other. No longer a Horde, but agents with a mission, we swarmed over the beach and into the dunes, wildly, separately, any way we could. Gangs of one, I thought. An army of gangs-of-one. Now or never. No turning back.

The god Naal is a vengeful god, a god of fire and ice. Fire, fog, sand; grey mist all around, lit with gouts of flame; shouting – a lot of shouting; panic, fear, confusion; fear of being alone; fear of friends, foe, *anyone* approaching through the mist; fear of not knowing what to do; fear of doing too much and getting a spear through the neck; fear of ambush; of losing your way; of fire, the unexpected, the expected, a confrontation, sudden arrows, an icy blade in the back. Fear. Of every-thing. This was what battle was like.

Fire and ice. Sand and mist. These were the colours of battle. The fog-banked morning was the morning *we'd* chosen, Naal help us. The wolf-headed god had yawned and scratched and coughed up a rolling pea-souper, wrapping us all in a closed-in world of grey and orange that fed into itself whichever way you tried to escape it. The same dunes loomed that had loomed before, the same panic jumped in my chest. Hadn't I been this way before? Where was I going, anyway? And where was the Leaderene?

Closing on the Pits from the beach-head with flaming brands of fire, the Leaderene, always a drama-queen, had made her move pretty late. No one knew what they were doing anyway, but the flares, seemingly coming from every direction at once, fired panic all round so everyone struck out wildly at everything they saw. Dimly I heard a whistle and headed towards it. The capture of Viger Wildgoose, I hoped, bundling him home in bonds already in my mind with the comfy thought that it might, after all, be all right. Bring on the hero's return, or even – especially – rollmop her-rings by the fire and an end to battles, always.

Someone thickened in front of me. I poised my ice-spear, waiting a second, on the hair-trigger edge of throwing it.

"Axes! For the Axes!" A blood-heavy voice, but a friend all the same.

"Who's there?" I peered. "That you, Arf?"

"It's me," said Vert heavily. Vert, and not-Vert. Vert bloodied, wild and sand-streaked. "I don't like it, Broddy."

"Hey," I reassured, "you'd have to be insane to like *this*. Seen the Leaderene? Know which way it's going?"

"I don't know and I don't care," said Vert brokenly. "I just almost killed my sister."

"You did *what*?"

"Nesta. She came in the advance. I came up behind her, almost hit her, I only just saw who she was in time, I almost – " He held up a finger and thumb. "Just that far away. Only just *that* far away from killing her, Broddy. Then I thought what I'd almost done anyway, and I never thought it would be this way an' I don't like it, Broddy, I don't care about the Pits nor none of it, I just want to go home – "

A couple of fighters clashed by in the mist, bashing and smashing each other with their clubs, ducking and striking, seeing nothing. I dimly recognized Gargas and Agerod, Argos' nephew. They had it all wrong. Couldn't they *see*? Why were they fighting each other? It probably wasn't the first time that the same side fought each other in battle, and it probably wouldn't be the last. The whole thing was truly insane; I hadn't realized how much. As if to underline it, a hunting horn sounded somewhere. Great. Everything *else* had gone wrong. Why not have the hunt return across the line of battle?

I pushed Vert down. "Hunt's coming. Duck."

The thunder and bell of the chase and the brothers Fingers – Stub and Falco at least, plus half a hundred dogs – rushed headlong over the dunes. Something maddened and wounded and very large indeed passed us close – very close – in the mist. Spears wagged in its sides. More than one in its neck.

I started up. "Ur!"

I raised a hand to stop them, but the Fingers ran right past me. Dogs flooded over and round me, even through my legs. Someone threw a spear. Someone else an axe.

"Wait!" I shouted, taking Vert's spear. "Call them off, you can't just – "

Ur's wondering, broken death-call echoed off the wide, uncaring lake, off the watching peaks and in the depths of Mended Vision, where cave-painted aurochs ages old listened uncaringly too.

The taste of blood filled my mouth. "Murder!" I screamed, running. "He's *always* been here! You don't understand! *Don't kill him!*"

15

Grub Fingers Gets a Haircut –
Honeyland-over-the-Mountain

I don't really know what happened after that, because then I started running. I ran in a straight line up and down and over and through everything, no matter what, up to and into Hayta. I think I was off my head.

Hayta stared. "Broddy! What are you doing?"

I looked at Hayta wildly. "Fighting to keep the peace."

"Fighting to keep the peace? What does that *mean*?"

My hands were shaking. I put down the Burial Committee hammer. "It means it's all gone wrong."

"Hunt's back," Hayta said, after a moment. "Looks like they made a big kill."

I wiped my eyes with the back of my arm. Then I said, "You know when I said I might go somewhere? I might go somewhere soon. There's nothing here for me now."

Hayta came close, then closer, not understanding, wanting to tell me something. "I came to find you. I wasn't sure if you knew – "

"Knew what?"

"The way they left, like they knew what they were doing, I thought you must've told them to meet you somewhere. I'd've stopped them if I thought – "

"Why don't you tell me what you're talking about?"

"Your sisters."

"What about them?"

"I think they went over the mountain."

The mist cleared briefly, making me a tunnel, showing me Viger Wildgoose bringing down his bloodaxe. I wondered who might be under it.

"Broddy? Didn't you hear what I said?"

So the Beast took her sisters over the mountain. *An me an' Bee's goin' if we want to.* Why didn't that surprise me? I could see Viger plainly through the mist. Maybe he couldn't see me. Suddenly he did. He paused as he brought down his bloodaxe on some pallid-looking driftwood.

"Yo Broddy!" The mist swirled. Viger was with us in a moment. "Broddy Brodson!" He threw down his axe and hugged me.

I shrugged him off angrily. "What's with the welcome? You off your head?"

"Hey," Viger said, "I thought you might be off yours."

"Stay back," I warned, behind my biggest

hafted dagger. I whipped out my whistle and blew the signal. "Stay back, I'm taking you in."

"It won't do you any good whistling," said Viger. "Arthagarth whistled before."

"I'm warning you, Wildgoose. No tricks."

Viger spread his hands. "Broddy. Why?"

"Why what?" I struggled with the feeling that it was good to see him and lost.

"I told your Leader the last time. That's an end to fighting."

"Right. That's why you're about to attack."

"Who's attacking?"

"*You* are. The Pits."

Viger shook his head.

It occurred to me something was wrong.

"Take a look around," said Viger. "Does it look like we're about to attack?"

I looked around. Dimly the sandpits showed me huddled forms under banks and in liquid-bottomed dugouts between the dunes. Winter had hit the Pits hard. Even Cud – I just about recognized Cud – even Cud was a sick-looking shadow of his former evil self. One or two stick-thin characters, including Spider, lay pathetically in a hollow half-buried by sand and snow. I had a feeling it would be the last long sleep some of them would ever take. I looked away, something like shame welling up.

"We want a better place to go," said Viger softly, "but it isn't Mended Vision. We've had enough, Broddy, there's nothing here for us now.

There's got to be something better, somewhere over –"

"Just a minute." I held up my hand. "Is Grub Fingers here?"

Someone cursed and yelped. The line of torch-bearers, ice-spear carriers and battle-weary liggers slowly crowding the dunes knotted briefly. Grub Fingers popped out of a scuffle like pus out of a spot. He dusted himself down, scowling. Then he looked at me craftily.

"What can we do for you, Broddy?"

"How about the truth, you lowlife."

"Ah, the truth. Who knows the truth in battle? Most regrettable, I'm sure we all –"

"Know what this slimeball did?" I asked the assembling crowd of Axes, Pits and hangers-on. "This sleaze came over and told us the Pits were about to attack. Any day, he told us. They'll wipe you out. Treat you bad. Take anything worth taking." I raised my voice to drive the point home. *We didn't want any more trouble. He's the only reason we're here.*"

"Now, then." Grub looked to left and right. "Some misunderstanding?"

"No misunderstanding. He told us the same thing," said Viger. "He told us the Axes were preparing for a *major* raid. Let them, I said. There's nothing worth stealing, anyhow. Know what he said?"

I watched Grub closely. "What did he say?"

"He said, you better watch out. They're killing

and eating people. That's when I posted a guard."

"That's disgusting." I dimpled Grub's chin with the business end of my biggest hafted dagger. "Guess who set us up? Always rich pickings off a battlefield, right Grub? Plenty of knives and shields and good plate leather to strip off dead bodies, am I wrong? War for profit. I'm interested. How does that make you *feel*?"

Grub sweated. "Makes me feel – kind of – "

"Dirty?" suggested Viger.

Grub spread his unconvincing fingers. "We all make mistakes, I – "

I took Grub by the topknot. "I love you, too," I told him. Then I chopped it off.

"Who wants to come, come! Honeyland-over-the Mountain!" I stood on the highest dune in the sandpits swinging the Burial Committee hammer over my head. "Over the mountain. With me. Everyone. Over the mountain – "

Viger Wildgoose met my eyes, taking up the chant, passing it on, his voice behind mine as solid as heart-of-oak. "Everyone. Everyone over the mountain. Everyone over – "

"The mountain." Eels joined in. "Honeyland-over-the – "

"Mountain." I swung the Burial Committee hammer in wider loops, and wider. "Everyone who wants to come, come. Good grazing. A better place. A better way to live. Honeyland – "

"Over the mountain. Everyone – " Cud smiled

weakly. "Everyone over – "

"The mountain."

"Who wants to come, come!"

"Honeyland-over-the-Mountain."

"A better way, a better place – "

"Good grazing."

"The best."

"Honeyland-over-the-Mountain."

"What do I tell Argos?" Hayta looked up sadly. We both knew the moment had come.

"Tell Argos I'll send him a message when we're settled."

"A message. When you're settled."

"Right."

"Anything else?"

"Tell him – tell him I'm sorry."

"Hope you find them quickly."

"We have to." I looked at the mountain. Somewhere up there were my sisters. "They won't last long up there."

"I should've done something to stop them, it's just – "

"Hey. No blame. You know?"

Hayta nodded dumbly. Then he hugged me like it was the last hug in the universe.

The breaking sun showed me Climbing Sky. The glacier under its south face blazed with lines of light. That would be the crevasses. Above the glacier a snow-bridge shaped like a swallow threw slanting blue shadows over the lowest, and nearest, snow-field. Way in the clouds somewhere above a second – maybe a third – snow-field, plus Naal alone knew what other obstacles, lay the ridge. The ridge which marked the way over. I looked at the mountain. Then I looked at Hayta. The last hug in the universe. Probably it was.

16

The Last of Ur – Climbing the Sky – The Snow-field

"Murder!" I screamed, running. "He's always been here! You don't understand! Don't kill him!"

No matter how many times I re-run Ur's death it still hurts like it happened yesterday, like everything *else* I relive over and over whether it helps or not, which it doesn't. But I have to deal with it now. There's no way I can skip it. Some memories belong to the lake, you know? You can't drag them over the mountain.

"Please don't kill him! You can't! Please wait!"

Remember I told you I didn't know what happened after the hunt – because when Ur rushed by in the mist I started running? It wasn't entirely true. The first part was mainly a blur. But the last part I remember too well. It took me a long time to get over Ur's death. Round about nine thousand years, if you want to know. I thought I might not be able to tell it at all. But I think I can handle it now.

I don't remember how I reached Ur ahead of the hunt, but I did. What I *do* remember is snatching Vert's poison spear and taking off like a madman. I ran for what seemed like a long time but probably wasn't – I think I was off my head – knowing, somehow, I had to get to him first. He was blundering way down on the lakeshore with up to a dozen spears in his back when I found him. Poor Ur. He didn't understand. He was practically on his knees by the time I reached him. I could hear the dogs flooding over the dunes in back of the lakeshore, baying for blood – Ur's blood. He turned as I reached him. He knew it was me. His liquid brown eyes met mine, not understanding, but trusting.

I vaulted on his back without stopping. Ur trembled. His sides heaved. I urged him into the lake with my knees. Ur crashed into the shallows. I took Vert's poison spear. I wiped three-minute poison in Ur's open jugular, whispering things I never told anyone else, ever, in my life. Ur's eye clouded in seconds. By the time we reached the pack-ice, Ur was going, going, gone. His body just drifted away in the cool green depths underneath me, peaceful as anything, leaving me swimming for my life. It was the first and last dip we ever had together. But it was a great swim. The best. I never felt so good about anything as when I splashed out in the hunt's face and shrugged and spread my hands.

"Don't bother," I told them. "Call off your dogs," I told them, "you won't find anything now."

Finally they called off their dogs and went home. They didn't like it much. Some were for dredging Ur out. Then I showed them Vert's spear. Ur would sleep in peace. No one would eat the earthbound spirit of the lake, not even the dogs. His flesh would be tainted with poison. Nine thousand years later, Needcliff would find him intact. But I didn't know that then.

"Snap out of it, Broddy." Viger nudged me impatiently. "Wake up. You're not with us, are you?"

I shuddered. "No. Just thinking."

"Climbing's not hard enough? You think *and* climb, you fall. Think about that, why don't you?"

Viger turned away. I heard him encouraging Dug to keep up. I sharpened up. He had every right to feel angry I was leaving it all up to him. We had around five hours' daylight left to locate my sisters before the temperature took a dive. We were out on an open glacier with little or no food and a half-starved bunch of stragglers behind us and nothing in front of us but a vague path through unknown dangers to the top of a moutain, and no guarantee anything waited on the other side except more of the same. I took a last, long look at the lake in the valley far below. Ur belonged to the lake. That was where I would leave him. I handed Viger a blood-warm drink of water. Surviving was quite hard enough.

"Thanks." Viger drank deeply, searching the snow-field ahead. "They're two hours ahead of us, tops. We've got to catch up with them soon."

I nodded slowly. "Think so?"

Viger narrowed his eyes. The tracks in the snow were good. So long as it didn't snow any more, the tracks would be easy to follow. I watched Viger weighing the signs. We'd made good time so far. Viger had led the way like he knew what he was doing. Hadn't he been shown a path over the mountain by the legendary Horl Stendevenger, no less? All the same, he'd followed the tracks. I didn't know, but I hoped, my sisters had gone the right way. How long could three small girls survive on the side of a mountain? How they got past the glacier was anyone's guess. Every crevasse we hopped over, Viger tensed and looked in, hoping not to see a small body smashed in the snow at the bottom. It was weighing on him heavily, I could tell. Time I was ready to share it.

"I'll take the lead now, if you like," I told him, stowing my drinking-bladder next to my skin so it wouldn't freeze. "Why don't you take a break?"

"No way." Viger tried a smile. It didn't come off too well. "Look up there and tell me what you see."

I looked up. "I see my sisters' tracks. I see the path. I see the beginning of the second snow-field."

"And?"

"And the snow-bridge we have to cross first."

Viger nodded. "Right. The snow-bridge we have to cross first. With this lot half-dead to start with. Without any mattocks or rope."

"My sisters did it."

"Let's hope."

Someone shouted. Straggling away below us, everyone turned to watch Arf. A fight had broken out over the cookpot that Arf had insisted on dragging behind him all the way from the sandpits. Probably Gargas' brother was insisting he leave it behind. I couldn't really blame him. Arf and his stupid porridge-pot were holding everyone up.

"Will you look at that?" Viger cupped his hands round his mouth. "Arf, you idiot! Put down that cookpot and leave it!"

Arf was a problem that day on the mountain, a problem growing worse with every step. He'd wanted a stop on the hour. Arf was pretty down-to-earth, for a mystic. If he couldn't see one step ahead, he'd sit on his hands and cook up a mess of porridge. Barley-meal porridge was one thing Arf had no sense of humour about at all.

He sat down as soon as he reached us. "Why can't we stop? My side hurts."

"I don't know about you, but I plan to get off this mountain." Viger looked severe. "We've got to get over the ridge before nightfall, yeah? Plus, we have to find Broddy's three sisters."

I looked at Arf. "What's the matter with you? You've been dragging your feet all the way."

"My side hurts," Arf said again.

The Leaderene examined Arf. I felt bad when I saw his side. Arf had actually been wounded in battle. Everyone else had got off pretty lightly. But not Arf. He *would*, I almost blamed him, stopping myself in time. It wasn't Arf's fault someone had taken a swing at him with a six-foot herring-pike. Three cracked ribs, said the Leaderene, feeling Arf's chest, purple from rib-cage to breastbone. More than enough to brag about.

"Plus my head," whimpered Arf, enjoying the examination. "My head hurts all the time."

"Get off it, Arf." Vert joined us. "No one's about to carry you home to bed."

I'd known the idea of crossing the mountain wasn't way off the planet when Vert threw in behind us. Vert looked after Number One. He wouldn't have come if he'd thought there was no chance at all. Those going over the mountain for the first and only time that bitter winter's day of 7650 BC included: Arf; me; Viger Wildgoose; Vert; Eels; Burin; Dug; Gargas' brother Rorcus (not Gargas himself – his band "Stain the Cave" was big around the lakes, explained Gargas. Their music would probably suffer); Leister the Bowman and Leister the Bowman's half-brother; the Leaderene; Agerod the Thrower; the (wrestling) sisters Stump; Berk; Bedgo; Turtlejuice. No Cud. Cud kindly volunteered to stay behind and die on account of being a burden and having a repellent personality. He felt it was the least he could do.

Treak himself had (quickly) blessed the expedition. We *were* in a hurry, I explained. He'd even given Eels his last-of-summer hat. She wore it squarely over both eyebrows, the pine-marten's feet around its edges swinging gently over her eyes as she walked, the kind of eyes you liked more, the better you got to know them. I watched her top the glacier, helping Dug. Pretty soon she came over. She looked up once at the long, blue shadows under the snow-bridge.

"So what're their names?" she asked me, folding a wad of birch gum into her mouth.

She offered me some. I shook my head. Eels was pretty gutsy. She wasn't about to admit that the way ahead over the delicate-looking snow-bridge turned her over; one reason I liked her so much.

"Sorry? Who?"

"Your sisters. Don't they have names, your sisters?"

"Oh. Broddha, Brodil, Berod. All versions of *Brod*. But that's not what they're *called*."

"What are they called?"

"Um, my dad used to call Broddha – that's my eldest sister – my dad used to call her Tiddler, I don't know why. That was a long time ago. My middle sister's called the Beast. Call her Brodil, she bites you. The littlest one's Bee, always has been."

"Don't you get tired of all being Brods underneath?"

"Underneath? I don't think so. What kind of question is that?"

"A silly question."

"Right."

Eels grinned. I grinned back. It didn't seem to matter what we said.

182

Viger gave the thumbs-up. Then he blew the signal. He waved both arms and pointed upwards – always up. Everyone moaned and shouldered whatever they'd brought and moved off, Arf last of all, wearing his porridge-pot on his head, for heaven's sake. We climbed the snow-field slowly – it wasn't too steep, just long – our tracks muddling together over my sisters' tracks and snaking away behind us. Not for the first time, I felt a ball of anger in my chest. Where *were* they? What did they think they were *doing*? How *could* they have done this to me?

We dipped into the shadows under the snow-bridge. Once we were hidden from the sun, the chill touched every one of us, mainly Arf. Arf had come mountaineering in stylish summer deerskins, a half-cape of plaited grasses plus deerskin shoes stuffed with more grass, warpaint, and not a lot else. I couldn't really blame him. We'd all come straight from the sandpits after a battle, grabbing whatever we could. We were all in the same canoe.

The snow-bridge looked hairy any way you looked at it. From underneath it looked like a vaulted ceiling of blue ice over-arching half the mountain. It was only as you finally came up level with its swallow-tail supports that you could see daylight winking through the powder snow on the top of the bridge itself. It wasn't as strong as it looked. Not nearly so strong as a spider's web in a storm.

Viger stepped onto the snow-bridge. The snow-bridge creaked a little. A tiny chute of powder snow whispered away into space. It was a straight drop down to the glacier, hundreds of metres below. You'd have time to think before landing. Viger stepped back off the snow-bridge. He adjusted his belt. At last he looked up.

"OK," he said, "who's first?"

17

Walking the Angel's Wing –
King Wolf

It was my sisters' foot-prints that did it. Bee-sized
foot-prints in the snow, right over that snow-
bridge and way up over on the other side. The
tracks in the snow were evenly-spaced, like they
hadn't hopped or hurried. Like they weren't really
worried at all. Bee's tracks stood out beside the
others, so small and neat and even they got right
to me. My four-year-old sister had crossed this
bridge like it was a picnic trip to the woods. What
was I, scared to follow?

"Anyone up for it?" Viger asked.

"Me. I'm leading, OK?" I stepped right up.
Almost onto that snow-bridge.

"Sure?"

"*My* sisters, aren't they? I'm leading. It's cool."

"I'll go first, if you like." I could see he didn't
want to. "There're no second chances, Broddy."

I grinned. "Were there ever?" It was as near to
brave as I got.

I straightened my furs and freed up my arms and swapped a few things around before I stepped out on to the snow-bridge. No sense making an untidy corpse. Was that it? Not quite. I ducked something off my neck and handed it over to Eels.

"Keep this for me, will you?"

Eels held it up. The amber bear spun on its thong. "Isn't this the pendant the Thrower took off Treak?"

"Argos?" I nodded. "He gave it to me before the hunt. Now I'm giving it to you."

"Hey, I don't want it. It's yours."

"Keep it, all right? Give it back on the other side, if you want. OK, I'm ready." Argos would've been proud of me. I turned to face the snow-bridge. "Right, if I make it over, I'll – "

"We'll know when you make it over." Viger shook his head. "I wish I could rope you up."

"You cross the mountain with your heart, right?"

"Right."

Viger grinned, surprised I remembered. Then he braced my arm. I put out one foot and leant on it. Viger leant out after me. I brought my other foot forward slowly. Viger let go. I held my breath. So far, so good. I was totally on the snow-bridge. It totally held my weight.

"Nice going, Broddy," Vert said.

"It would be, if I'd gone anywhere," I told him.

Another step. And another. Each step, my foot sank in the sugar-snow and something underneath it creaked. Each step, a trickle of snow whispered away into space. But I didn't mind. It was all so drop-dead beautiful. I'm sure my mouth was open. You couldn't not feel small, the way the bridge curved around under the blue-shadowed face of the mountain with the glacier miles below and tons of ice and snow, just hanging, you know, like a wing or a curtain or something. I was walking along an angel's wing, I swear. That snow-bridge was a beautiful thing, probably the most beautiful thing I'd ever seen in my life.

"Way to go, Broddy!" Vert shouted.

Halfway across already. I could see the end of the bridge now. One swallow-tail arch flicked away to an ice-shelf. The other swept up onto the second snow-field. A snow-trickle hissed off the bridge. It wouldn't have been so bad, but there were places ahead where I could actually see daylight through little holes pitting the surface. With every step I could hear snow falling off the underside of the snow-bridge, detaching itself from that vaulted blue ceiling I was walking over and powdering away in space.

Don't look down. Keep walking on air. Don't even think about how fragile the bridge really is. One small step – and another. So many things to think about. Look at that ice-wall. Those hanging blue curtains of ice. *Think you know the ice? Not the ice. Myself.* Waterfalls, curtains, feathers of ice. Stunning, or what? Amazingly, stunningly –

"Keep left," Viger warned. "I don't like the look of that – "

Something cracked. My leg shot down through the bridge with a tearing sound and a thump.

"All right, Broddy? Broddy, you all right?" Someone screamed. Not me.

I waggled my leg. It was just my leg that had gone through. No reason I couldn't pull it out. My head ached. Points of light swam around in front of my eyes. Everything looked kind of cock-eyed. *Was* I all right? Up to my thigh in a snow-bridge? Halfway up a mountain in winter? And that wasn't all. I started to laugh. Maybe I was snow-blind. Maybe I was mad. But it looked to me like a wolf on the bridge. A big old shaggy Arctic wolf, grinning from ear to ear. A wolf on an angel's wing. Why was it looking at *me*?

Was it *ever* looking. The tension between us seemed like it was holding up the bridge itself, or maybe even the mountain. I absolutely knew I couldn't lose it. OK, King Wolf, watch me now. I pulled my leg up out of that ice-hole like my life depended on it. King Wolf turned. Hey, don't go! I got up and I followed him over the bridge, just like that, without thinking.

But when I got over, he was gone. No sign of any wolves on the slope above. Only a line of tracks, wandering off in the snow. I was still wondering if I'd really seen him and where he'd gone if I had, when Viger showed up at my elbow. I jumped, I really did. I actually left the ground.

"Viger! How'd you go?"

"No sweat, once we found the weak spot."

"Once *I* found the weak spot, you mean."

"Dunno how you got out of that one, Broddy. I thought you were – "

"Dead meat? Thanks."

I handed Vert off the snow-bridge. He gave me an eyebrow. *So* kind. Eels smacked my hand away, grinning. Arf and Duggie followed. I handed Arf off the snow-bridge. I rapped him on his cookpot-head. "Arf. Anything cooking in there?"

The others crossed one by one, maybe fifteen in all. Agerod the Thrower walked stiffly in the rear. I felt a bit anxious, watching him cross. Wasn't the very last person always the one to fall? But Argos' nephew didn't fall. What he did was, he stamped. Three sharp stamps and a quick hop off it, and the snow-bridge shuddered, hung a moment, then slumped away with a sound like collapsing mammoths.

"Unbelievable." Vert stared. "What did you do *that* for? Now we can't go back."

Agerod shrugged. "Not about to, are we?"

"Someone might want to, sometime."

"Nah. Do or die, mate, you know?" Agerod grinned. He looked a lot like Argos.

The second snow-field stretched away to the ridge. Viger and I sized it up. Nothing but jumbled rock. Past mid-day already. How much further to go?

"Looks kind of spooky up there." Viger shaded his eyes and squinted as far as he could. "Pretty

189

rough ground. Worst thing is, no tracks."

"No tracks?"

"Not over rocks like this. No way of telling which way your sisters went. See that notch in the ridge up there? That's where we're headed. The only way over, so far as I know."

I looked. I thought I could see a dip in the ridge. Maybe that was what he meant. The thought of going over any dip in any ridge anywhere without my three sisters made me feel sick to my stomach. I hadn't let myself think about that. The idea that *I might not find them* began to firm up around me, like something you couldn't prevent no matter what you did. I didn't let Viger know what I was thinking. Saying I was worried that I might not ever see my sisters again might help to make it real.

Instead I said, "Ever see a wolf as big as that before?"

"What wolf?"

"Don't give me that. You know. King Wolf, out on the snow-bridge. I can't explain how, but he kind of made me get up."

Viger looked at me.

"You didn't see that huge great snow-wolf? Standing in the shadows on the bridge?"

Viger shook his head. "Way too high for wolves up here. They don't go much above the tree-line in winter."

"This one did."

"Maybe." I could see he didn't believe me.

Gargas' brother picked something up. "What *is*

this stuff? Mammoth bone or something?"

"I dunno, it's everywhere." Something rattled, way up the slope. A slope of bones, I thought. I threw back my head and shouted. *"Broddha! Bee! Where are you?"* It didn't seem very loud. I'd just cupped my hands around my mouth to yell up the slope again, when Viger knocked them away.

"For the love of Naal, Broddy. Want to bring the whole snow-field down on top of us? Shout like that again, we're dead."

"What *is* it with this Naal stuff? It's just Arf of course, but now *everyone's* getting into it. Naal this, Naal that, it makes me sick, even Mum–" I stopped. I was shaking. I felt like hitting someone. "Arf made it all up ages ago. There's no such god as Naal."

"Worried about your sisters, aren't you?" Viger sat me down on a pile of bones.

"Wouldn't you be? Now I can't even *call* them."

"It's disgusting." Gargas' brother threw down a bone. "What is this, the elephant's graveyard?"

"Isn't it obvious?" Eels pitched a bone in the air. We watched it fall, turning over and over and over, all the way down to the glacier, until we couldn't make it out any more.

"What's obvious?" asked Duggie.

"Where we are." Eels sighed. "Bones? On Climbing Sky Mountain? Could it be – "

What else? The Laying-out Ground of the Dead.

18

Arf Puts His Foot Down –
The Snow-hole

"I guess it never mattered much, anyway."

"What didn't?"

"Who had the sandpits."

"No." I didn't feel much like talking. "Just so somebody did."

"They weren't *that* great to start with. It's funny, but you always want what someone else has, don't you?"

I nodded. Eels was right. In the relief after the snow-bridge, everyone but me had lightened up. Not easy, in a graveyard. The Laying-out Ground of the Dead wouldn't be high on my list of fun places. If you didn't mind spooky, it wasn't so bad. The wind was just about the worst thing. Moaning and whistling between stacks of old bones, it set everyone's nerves on edge. But it made a change, walking somewhere (fairly) solid, even if the bones *did* have a way of suddenly ratcheting down the slope and taking you with them.

A line of drunk-looking skulls watched us pass. I guessed they didn't have too much to say about it. The odd almost-complete skeleton surprised us, probably recent additions. The snow-covered heaps of really ancient bones were a disgrace, clucked Arf. The Burial Committee should've seen 'em buried, soon as they were clean. That was the whole point. Some bones were old, some not-so-old. Some were smooth and intact under the snow. Others lay smashed where the kites had dropped them, in gruesome-looking piles. Probably Uncle Jungleboots' kneebones, or Auntie Squimmidge's ribs, who cared? Bones were bones. Picked clean, stacked high. Those who'd once moved them had long ago Climbed the Sky.

"This place gives me the creeps," Eels said. "I wish the wind would stop."

"Talking about the sandpits – "

"What about them?"

"I remember, I came over and spied on you once."

"And?"

"It was about three days after you first turned up. Viger was sitting in a pile of shellfish. You and Burin were talking about – " I stopped, embarrassed.

"Murdering Treak?" Eels tossed Treak's hat. "I remember."

"Remember the day he marked his boundaries? Those smelly sticks in the path?"

"I almost forgot." Eels took off the amber bear.

"Here you go. Take this back."

"Keep it."

"Really?"

"Really."

"Cool." Eels looped it over her head. The amber bear sat snugly on her breastplate. As good a place as any to be, and probably better than most.

I felt like I was leaving a part of myself in the graveyard with every step I took. The feeling got worse and worse, the further up we went. When at last we reached the top and no one had fallen in the bones or got too badly spooked or discovered they were stepping in Granny Snatchpacket's remains, I turned and looked back helplessly at the Laying-out Ground of the Dead. The light was dying already. We weren't going to find them, I knew. Only one shot to find them. One afternoon on the mountain. Nightfall would see us over the ridge or frozen, wherever my sisters were. You didn't mess with the mountain. It was pretty unforgiving to those caught out overnight.

Arf set down his cookpot under the ridge. "That's it. I'm stopping here." He brought out dry sticks from his satchel and cleared a space for a fire.

Viger nodded carefully. "OK." He turned to announce the halt. "All right, folks. Ten minutes. Then we're over the ridge."

Over the ridge. Ten minutes. The very top of Climbing Sky looked down over the blue-shadowed ridge that rolled along its back like a wave.

The notch in its edge – the way over the mountain – seemed obvious now. No footprints led there. Nothing.

"What can I say?" Viger knelt beside me. "I'm really sorry, Broddy. I can't risk everyone, looking. You never know, they might've – "

"Might've fallen after the snow-bridge? After the tracks disappeared? Nice one, Viger. I didn't even think about that."

"That wasn't what I meant."

"What did you mean?"

"Just – nothing."

Viger moved away. I'd've moved away from me if I could. No one could really help me, even if Arf thought he could.

"Sure you lit a big enough fire, Arf?" Vert folded his arms. "What are we, setting up camp?"

"Broddy needs porridge. Isn't that right, Broddy?" Arf's quick fire licked up. He undid his pouch of barley meal. He threw a couple of hand-fuls into his cookpot, already broiling snow.

"That's right." I looked at Arf gratefully. Maybe I did need porridge.

"Don't unpack things, OK?" Viger went round warning everyone. "Just a quick break, all right? Temperature's dropping all the time."

I ate my porridge slowly. It gave me a chance to look around. A chance to believe we finally almost crested Climbing Sky. It was hard to believe we were anywhere but a floating snow-cone in space. The land of the lake had drowned under clouds so thick they looked and felt like a sea. It was easy to forget who you were, up on that ridge with the crow's-nest peaks swimming in mist like the tip-top crown of a giant. Whatever happened afterwards, could anything follow this? Climbing a mountain was like unfolding a story. Like climbing into yourself. It was dangerous, exciting, a loner's game. It made me feel alive. The feeling out on the angel's wing. The feeling once you got over it. I couldn't explain how I felt about it, but I knew I'd discovered something. Climbing was something special for me. This was just the start.

It was then that I felt him watching me. That tension no one could break. Hey, King Wolf. I see you, way along the ridge under that glassy-looking overhang, a lone white wolf in a strange-shaped platform of light, looking at me, *looking*. I hear you, King Wolf. What is it? I'm coming. OK.

"What did I tell you?" Viger hassled Arf. "*Don't unpack*. How long d'you think we're staying?"

"Don't care," mumbled Arf. "Not going anywhere anyway."

"What did you say?"

Arf looked up. "I'm staying here, all right?"

King Wolf *looked*. I got up carefully. "Viger, don't move. Turn around slowly. See him now?"

Viger turned. "See who?"

"Go to him, Broddy." Arf's face lit up. "Can't you see he wants you?"

I knew he'd be gone when I got there. By the

196

time I scrabbled over the blue-shadowed slope to the place under the overhang where King Wolf had sat perfectly on a perfect platform of light, the only thing there was the snow-hole he'd been marking. *Got something to tell me, King Wolf? I believe you do. Oh, yeah.* I couldn't dig it out fast enough. The snow-hole caved in under me. It was filled with arms and legs. Hard, steamy, wriggling arms and legs and heads and elbows and someone crying *You're hurting me, get off!*

I don't know what I said. Probably something like, "It's me, get up! Get up, get up, it's me!" – or something twice as original. The Beast surfaced crossly through powder snow. I felt a bit desperate. There was a real danger I could suffocate my sisters just as I'd found 'em, now I'd collapsed the snow-hole. The Beast thought so, too. "Look what you've done! You've squashed it all down! Now it'll *never* – "

I grabbed the Beast's head and planted a big sloppy wet one right between her eyes, about the first and only time I'd ever kissed her. That stopped her. "Yuk." She wiped her forehead disgustedly. Then she helped Broddha out.

I hauled Bee, blubbering, out of a tangle of red arms and legs. She looked like a half-drowned kitten.

"I t'ant breathe, I t'ant breathe – "

"Shush," I soothed, "can now. Look, you're out. It's me."

Bee looked at me tearfully. "Argos be back."

197

"Not Argos. Will I do?"

Bee nodded hard up and down. Big drops of water spilled down her cheeks. I stopped them with my finger. I couldn't bear to lose a single one. "Don't. Everything's going to be all right now. Promise." I hugged her very hard.

Finally I saw everyone was safe. Then I started feeling angry. So angry, I could've pushed them all right back in that snow-hole all over again. It was mainly the Beast I wanted to push in the snow-hole.

"This your idea? Why are you *in* this snow-hole? Your idea to come up the mountain, was it?"

"Found us, din' you?" The Beast's jaw trembled very slightly. "I *tol'* them after you went in battle you'd come up the mountain and meet us."

"Why?" I squeezed her arm. "Why would I want to do that?"

"Because."

"Because what?"

The Beast's eyes filled up. "Because you'd Climb the Sky like Mum 'n' Dad."

It ran so deep, there was no answer. I turned on Broddha instead.

"I can't believe you came up here. You know you'd have frozen to death if I hadn't found you? You'd be frozen *now* if you hadn't found a snow-hole."

"We didn't find it. We dug it." Broddha flushed.

"Whatever. How come you left the cave in the first place? What did you think you were *doing*?"

Broddha's face crumpled. She pointed to the Beast. "*She* said. You told her. You'd meet us. An' I never. Thought it'd. Be like. This an' I'm sorr-ee."

"We saw Naal," the Beast said. "That's how we knew to dig a snow-hole."

"You saw Naal. Right."

"Big wolf." Bee made him big with her hands. "Big wolf stay an' keep us warm."

I looked at Broddha. I looked at Bee. I didn't know what to make of it all, who would? The facts were, the snow-hole high on the ridge had protected my sisters pretty well. My sisters knew nothing about survival, climbing, or keeping warm in the snow. They could have frozen to death or got lost as easily as falling off a mountain, always the other main option. They might have gone any way after the snow-bridge, any way under the ridge. But they hadn't. Instead, they'd stopped and dug a snow-hole. Something had told them to stay where they were and keep warm. I looked up. The ice-shelf overhang glittered under a blizzard sky. Maybe the wolf-headed god was looking down behind it. *Thanks a million, King Wolf, Great Naal, whatever your other names are. Thanks for watching over them.*

"Anyway, we're all together now," I comforted, giving up. "And we better get a move on. See the others?"

The others waved on the ridge. Come on, come on, come on! The soon-come peak of Climbing Sky lowered over the notch that marked the way.

Viger's path had been steady. Honeyland waited on the other side. It really wasn't far.

"Where are we going?" asked the Beast.

I winked and pointed. "Up 'n' over, guess where?"

The Beast took a sharp breath. "*Really*?"

"Really."

Then she jumped up, shouting. "I guess! I guess! I guess!"

19

Alias the Iceman

I've still got the Burial Committee hammer. At least, I know where it's buried. Old Nerdcliff'd probably give his right arm for an Anglo-Maglemosian ceremonial hammer. Pity he'll never find it.

I expect you'd like to know what happened over-the-mountain. What I did with the rest of my life. OK. We made it. The legendary Horl Stendevenger himself welcomed us into a new Tribe of Families on the other side, which wasn't a whole lot different from the side we'd left behind. There wasn't much Honeyland about it. Honey, let me tell you, was in pretty short supply. We never worried too much, Eels and I. And we never called all our children Brod. We called our eldest girl Freya, our eldest boy Chert, and all the rest of 'em names of shrubs.

Argos visited most summers for the Throwing Open, walking around the mountain and meeting Horl Stendevenger halfway. He and Horl Stendevenger had a few friendlies first. Usually Argos brought Hayta with him. Hayta thickened as time went on. So did the snow-bridge on Climbing Sky. One winter it grew so strong Hayta brought his kids over it. They stayed a week and played with mine. It was enough to make anyone's eyes water.

What happened to Arf? I think you know that by now, but I'll join the dots anyway if you want. Back to the snow-ridge a moment. I can't put my finger on the moment I realized Arf was going to stay there; it kind of crept up on me slowly. It's creepy, I know, but I think Arf knew his fate, he really did. He kept getting glimpses, and all of them told him this was the spot. This mountain. This ridge. This fate. Oh, he played at having to mend his axe. He stirred his porridge and stuck out his chin. But there was a whole lot more to it than that.

"Come on, Arf, we're waiting," Viger had shouted from the ridge. "There isn't much daylight left."

"You go on. I'll catch you up." Arf stirred his porridge-pot grimly.

I left my sisters with the others. I ran back down to him fast. I took his spoon. I stood him up. I tried, I really did. "Arf. We're going. You've got to come *now*."

"In a minute. I've got to clean out this pot."

With both hands I seized Arf's porridge-pot. It was really hot. I didn't need much encouragement to fling it away off the ridge. "Now you don't have to. Come on."

Sadly Arf watched his cookpot bounding away down the slope. It jumped off a rise and crashed away in the mist. Arf unsheathed his axe and sat down. He fiddled the hemp fixings loose between the shaft and the blade. He didn't look up. His lips were blue, I noticed. So were his arms and legs. I think it was then that I realized Arf wasn't going to come, no matter what I said. No one could carry him off the mountain if he didn't want to go. Short of dragging Arf by the hair, there was nothing I or anyone else could do to make him change his mind.

"Arf." One more try. Make it count. "Arf, I want you to come. Do it for me. Please."

Arf struggled with himself. At last he got up. "I'm sorry, Broddy." Arf's face opened. I never noticed before how clear and blue his eyes were. "I'm sorry, Broddy, I can't. Not without mending my axe."

We looked at each other a long time. "No," I told him, finally. "No, I suppose not. But Arf – "

"What?"

"At least dig a snow-hole. You can't just stay here on the ridge."

"Yes," said Arf, "I can."

"If you don't – if you change your mind, I'll wait."

Arf's young-old eyes creased. "You might wait a long time, Broddy."

You might wait a long time, Broddy. And I have. Waited a long time to tell you this, I mean. We never found his body, once the snows had covered it up. Arthagarth Haagerbarta froze in the night and lay on that ridge nine thousand years, until the climate warmed and the snows finally drew back and the Archaeologist's Daughter brushed away ice from his orange leather brow. Famous at last. Poor old Arf, I think he saw it all in some strange way. Tall and weird and gifted, talking in tongues and not quite the full biscuit, the boy Haagerbarta truly broke the mould. I miss him, I really do.

Most winters over-the-mountain we thought about Arf. When Arf's spirit whistled high in lonely rifts we listened and heard the future in its voice. *Good grazing, good fishing, good fortune. One life, many mysteries. Enjoy.* We did things differently, over-the-mountain. We gave up killing aurochs, for starters, and we didn't send Olds to live apart. Instead, we kept 'em with us and treasured them for what they knew. Me, I hung on making the family wait on me hand and foot until I finally Climbed the Sky aged sixty-one, a pretty good innings for an old Pre-Boreal bloater.

After the kites cleaned my bones I slept a long time, woke up and found myself a ghost. There wasn't any in-between state to think it over. No asking, How'd you like to wake up a ghost and re-live it all from day one? It just happened. Asleep, then not-asleep. Why did I get to be a (young) ghost and no one else? I put it down to that last-of-summer of 7650 BC, the last-of-summer my feelings ran wild, the last-of-summer before the winter

I learned my life's passion, climbing. (I did a lot of climbing over the next few years, one reason the kites found my often-fractured bones easy meat.) Plus I wanted to set the record straight so badly, this story *had* to come through. Any way you look at it, this story's got to rile Nerdcliff. I hope it sticks in his throat 'til he coughs up a whole bunch of his phlegmy old theories and finally sees they say more about *him* than prehistory. It's partly why I'm telling it. The way I feel about archaeologists getting things wrong's enough to get *anyone* out of bed. Anyway. Next time you read prehistory or take a walk in the snow, remember the orange bag of bones on the ridge and the spook who filled you in about the way it could have been, should have been. The way it really was.

The Archaeologist's Daughter circled the office. She stopped beside the French technician. The French technician looked up.

"Gerard. Did you – did you write a story on the office computer?"

Gerard frowned. "A story?"

"About the iceman. About how he was really, like, psychic or something. He saw it all coming. That's how he ended up on the ridge. There's a long story under PITS.DOC – I thought it might be a joke."

Gerard shrugged. "I regret, but I not."

"Only it's got me in it and Dad in it and *every-thing*. It's really weird. Plus these Stone Age gangs fight each other over the sandpits. It's really bugging me who wrote it."

She wandered over to her father. The eminent archaeologist didn't look up.

"Did you, Dad?"

"Did I what?"

"Write that weird story on the computer."

Simps coughed drily without looking up. "I hardly think, Anna, I have time for writing stories when I have so much work to do – "

"All right. You don't have to tell me like that."

"Haven't you any school-work to do?"

"Plenty. Don't let me stop you working."

J.S. Needcliff looked up at last. "What's got into you lately?"

"Nothing. Everything. I don't know."

"No, I really don't think you do."

The Archaeologist's Daughter turned away. "I hate the way you never really listen."

"What's that?"

"Broddy Brodson's father never listened. He got drunk and fell in the cook pit. Might as well not even *have* one."

"Anna. You're rambling. Have what?"

"A dad, if he's never around. Anyway, I don't even *care* who wrote the story, it's all just like I thought it was, except Arf."

"I'm sorry – Arf?"

"The iceman. That's what's saddest about it. He wasn't a hero at all. Or maybe he was, in a way. It's such a shame. It's all a bit pathetic."

The Archaeologist considered his daughter. For the first time in a long while, he saw her for what she was. Full of needs and uncertainties, she had more claim on him than the past had. Perhaps he'd neglected her lately. Certainly he had.

Needcliff got up stiffly. "I think," he said, taking out his car keys, "I think we might go somewhere special for dinner tonight. Time we treated ourselves. Gerard – will you lock up?"

Later that night, they looked in again. When the lab had finally settled and the filters had slowed to a ten-minute drip and the cultures had bloomed in their dishes, Needcliff snapped on the light and ran his eyes over the office shelves for some report he'd forgotten. Then he clipped briskly off down the aisles to some other place he might have left it.

The Archaeologist's Daughter considered Arf. The iceman lay in his sterile cell as usual. He'd missed the wine and jokes over dinner, the closeness that came with breaking ice so long unbroken it felt like floating in a warm sea, a sea that would always support you. The iceman didn't have a father so clever his name was known in three continents, a father who wrote books and lectured at home and abroad. Poor iceman. He didn't have a lot to say for himself. Norbert, Arthagarth, Fred, Uther, the iceman – who *was* he, really? All of them, maybe. All of them and more. The Archaeologist's Daughter pressed her face to the glass and misted a circle. She tapped the glass once, twice, and decided. The Archaeologist's Daughter opened a cubicle door. She approached the bank of switches beside Arf's cell. She hesitated a moment. Arf's support systems winked and hummed, livelier than he was.

The Archaeologist's Daughter looked up. Her eyes had a look of Ur's. She flipped off the switches, tik-tok. Humidity control, off. Air filters, off. Temperature regulator, off. Tik-tok, tik-tok, tik-tok.

Anna Mae Needcliff, don't!

"Sleep well, Arf," she whispered, flipping off the light.

Her footsteps died with Needcliff's. The filters dripped every ten minutes, the cultures bloomed in their dishes on neatly-labelled shelves. Arf slumbered on in his shrink-wrap, decaying ever-so-slightly. The process would be irreversible by morning, as bacterial infection set in. I had to admire her. The Archaeologist's Daughter had done what time had failed to do. Arf would finally perish.

All Arf's gods looked down. Naal, Imchat, the false god Bol, the god before the false god Bol named Tek, the god before Tek named Kachu-Kaneachu. Naal and Imchat, Bol and Tek. All Arf's gods smiled down. I like to think – don't you? – I like to think he joined them.